Me and Me

Me and Me

Alice Kuipers

KCP Loft

KCP Loft is an imprint of Kids Can Press

Text © 2018 Alice Kuipers

Kids Can Press gratefully acknowledges the financial support of the Government of Ontario, through the Ontario Media Development Corporation for our publishing activity.

Published in the U.S. by Kids Can Press Ltd.
25 Dockside Drive, Toronto, ON M5A 0B5

Kids Can Press is a Corus Entertainment Inc. company

www.kidscanpress.com
www.kcploft.com

The text is set in Minion Pro and Optima

Edited by Kate Egan
Designed by Emma Dolan

Printed and bound in Altona, Manitoba, Canada in 6/2018 by Friesens Corp.

MIX
Paper from
responsible sources
FSC
www.fsc.org   FSC® C016245

US 18 0 9 8 7 6 5 4 3 2 1
US PA 18 0 9 8 7 6 5 4 3 2 1

Library and Archives Canada Cataloguing in Publication

Kuipers, Alice, 1979–, author
Me (and) me / Alice Kuipers.

Previously published: Toronto, Ontario : HarperTrophyCanada, 2017, ©2017.
ISBN 978-1-5253-0037-0 (hardcover)
ISBN 978-1-5253-0141-4 (softcover)

I. Title. II. Title: Me and me.

PS8621.U38M43 2018   jC813'.6   C2017-906777-X

To my sister, Anneke.
Far away but always near.

Prologue

My birthday: morning

"I like surprises," I say, as I strap myself in.

Alec turns his dark gaze to me. "Good. You ready?" He seems folded into his blue pickup, huge in the front cab.

"I think I'm ready. I, uh, I noticed the canoe." And the orange roses between our seats, filling the space with their heady scent.

Alec jars the truck into drive. I glance at his silver thumb ring and notice the way the cuffs of his rolled-up sleeves are slightly dirty, as if he's been hauling stuff or doing yardwork. I love his outdoorsy look, his clothes from those stores where they have tents set up in the back room. Makes him look like he's ready to chop down trees or build a fire. I can feel every movement of his foot on the pedals, the way his hands hold the wheel. I want his hands on me like that.

"Those are for you." He juts his chin toward the roses and smiles over at me.

"Thanks." I lift them to my nose. They smell of summer and of the past. A reel of the cemetery plays in my head.

Lucy:
Where are u?

Lark:
???

Lucy:
Breakfast, right?
B4 I work?
I was going to practice tarot reading
on u for ur birthday ...

She sends a photo of herself at D'Lish, where we both work. Her strawberry-blond hair is done in loose braids. She's pulling a pouty, sad face.

Lark:
Sorry!!! Going on a date.

Lucy:
Now? Who with???

Lark:
Last-minute decision.
Alec messaged last night.
He brought a canoe. Forgive me ;-)

Lucy:

Alec Sandcross? Nice!

I know how you feel about birthdays but 17 is a BIG DEAL

Lark:

Stop!

Lucy sends a Snap of herself sticking out her tongue.

Lark:

Tonight instead? Meet me and the band.

They have something planned.

Lucy:

I'm already coming after work.

Txt me later.

As Alec drives, he bites his bottom lip, which is pierced in the center with a silver stud. Cute habit. I've seen him do it in class when he's figuring something out. He's thoughtful in class like that, intense almost. But not broody. He's spontaneous, but not crazy. Relaxed, yet passionate about the things he loves. Last week in English he started talking about a book on climbing he was into: *Touching the Void.* I bet everyone is going to read it now. I pick at the meant-to-be-there rip in my pastel-green jeans. My leather boots come close to the knee. My pale shirt has tiny pink flowers peeping out from beneath my long black hair, which is loose.

He pulls onto the highway, and soon the city falls away. "I think you're going to enjoy today."

The prairies stretch out like a vast ocean before us. I drum my hands on my knees to the radio — Seafret — and then I'm thinking in lyrics: *Wanna give your heart to me. The fire in the woods, one tree ...* I note the words on my cell. I glance at Alec. I wonder if he's aware I mentally left the vehicle and traveled into a song. I wonder if he's thinking about me like I'm thinking about him. I wonder if he's noticed what I'm wearing.

"So, you canoed before?" He checks his rearview mirror and overtakes a car in front of us.

The song tugs at me. "I've got a lyric idea. Sorry. Can I just finish this?"

"Oh ... sure." Alec falls quiet, hand on the wheel as he stares ahead.

The words are flowing. Sometimes it happens like that, and a whole song appears where seconds before there was nothing. Whenever this happens on a date, boys think it's a challenge.

They want my full attention. But Alec just drives. Time flashes by. It's as if I've dived into deep water and I'm exploring a coral world, blue and beautiful. There's a psychologist we learned about recently who talks about *flow*. I get it when I'm in the zone like this. I only emerge when Alec pulls the truck into the lot at Pike Lake.

Songs almost never appear all at once. This one came out fully formed, so I'm feeling a little pumped.

"All done?" he says, turning off the ignition.

"Yeah. Sorry about that."

"It's cool. But now that you're done, let's go." He grins, unfolds himself from the truck and shuts his door.

I jump out, too. The lot fronts the beach, a thin strip of sand that runs along the tree line for three hundred yards or so. Beyond the beach is the silk-calm lake. I breathe in deeply, meditating on the clear view. The fresh breeze gives me goose bumps.

The place is almost deserted. Through a line of pine trees, I spot a couple and a small, blond child. I realize that it's the Fields family. He's *the* Martin Fields of Fields Studios, which is why I took a babysitting job with them six months ago. Except he was always at work so I hardly saw him. Whatever. I fell in love with his little girl and worked for them for about two months, before they decided to hire a full-time nanny instead.

"Annabelle?" I yell.

She turns and whoops but then pauses, as if suddenly shy. Suzanne — her mom — pushes her wild, curly hair from her face and waves hello. She walks over. Annabelle follows.

"Hi, Lark." Annabelle tips up her chin. "I'm nearly five now."

"Wow! You grew up. Soon you'll be older than me!" I count to five.

She giggles, and her blue eyes meet mine.

"Want to help me load the cooler?" Alec calls from the back of the truck.

Suzanne nods toward their two canoes, which are already at the edge of the lake. "We're hitting the water, too."

"Come find us out there."

"Mom?" Annabelle asks.

"Of course. Though I'm not sure we should disturb your privacy."

I smile. "No, come and find us on the water. Seriously. Sorry, Alec, I'm coming." A gust of cool wind ripples the water. I wave to Annabelle. Across the beach, Martin is still talking on his cell.

Back at the truck, I heft the cooler with Alec, the weight straining my muscles. "What are we eating?"

"By the end of the day," he says, "you'll be awestruck by my gourmet cooking skills. Now, help me get the canoe off the top."

We carry the canoe down to the water. Then suddenly I'm diving back into the song I was writing. One of the opening lines would work better if I added a word near the end to change the rhythm: *Wanna give your heart to me, the fire in the woods, cut down, cut down, just one tree ...* We slide the canoe into the water. It *thunks* against the sandy ground, and cold water slops over my pant leg.

"I've ... I'll just be a moment, promise." I take my cell out of my back pocket.

"Okay. If you want. But I'm going to show you something amazing." Alec waggles his eyebrows.

"Is this 'something amazing' out on the lake or something you can do?"

"I am indeed talented —" he winks to show he's kidding "— but no ... no, you write your song."

I tuck my phone away. "This better be good," I say, smiling.

A gull swoops overhead, a long way from the ocean. I pull off my shoes and socks. The icy water makes me gasp. The canoe wobbles as I climb in to join him and slip on my life jacket. The bottom of the canoe is hot from being in the sun on the roof of the car. The temperature contrast on my feet unfurls something in my chest. I ease fully into the moment.

"I wish I could sing," Alec says. "It must be awesome to be able to express yourself like that."

I love that he's curious about me. "Everyone can sing," I say.

"Not true."

"Okay." I sit on the front bench and turn back to Alec. "Not *exactly* true. But what I mean is that everyone can do *something* well. My mom taught me that." There she is. My mom. Even when I forget all about her, she's still watching over me. She left me a video. In it she tells me she's *always there*. Once I wrote a song with that as the hook.

Alec passes me a paddle, and I dip it into the water. The sound of the splash makes me think of ice cream, of summer, of holidays on the lake when I was a kid. In mutual but not uncomfortable quiet, we head along the shore of the lake. When I glance back at Alec, he smiles languidly. My heart does a pancake flip. Alec points out a beaver gliding by in the shallows.

A little while later, he interrupts the silence: "My dad used to take me on the water. He thought fishing was good for — I don't know — turning me into a man. 'Cept, I hated it, which drove him insane. I couldn't stand being cooped up in a small space — I wanted to swim, kept jumping in. Disturbing the fish. He used to yell at me, which was … well, not exactly relaxing."

He steers the canoe toward a small inlet, where the reeds hide us. His voice floats forward to me.

"We don't go on the water together anymore. And it's weird, but without him around, I don't mind the small space. Maybe that's because you're here."

We both stop paddling and let the canoe drift. My paddle drips freezing water over my knees. I swivel so I can see him. He leans his head to one side and smiles. His paddle is still in the water, and he occasionally re-angles it, making a deep ripple.

I point at the piercing in his lip. "Did it hurt?"

"I was, like, thirteen. I got into trouble. Big trouble. Call it rebellion."

"You seem like a good student. Into nature and stuff, not drugs and parties."

"Not that sort of rebellious." He places his paddle across the canoe and rests both arms on it. "So, have you canoed much before?"

"We canoed and camped every weekend during the summer when I was little. Dad doesn't look like it now." Alec stays quiet while I speak. "He has a heart thing, so he can't really exercise now. It means he's put on some weight, and he isn't so outdoorsy anymore, although he loves yardwork."

"What sort of a heart thing?"

"They don't really know. If he runs or gets his pulse up, I guess, his heart kinda skips."

My heart is skipping now. I don't want to talk about this. But I say, "It sucks. Some sort of scarring, maybe. I always think it's a broken heart 'cause of my mom." I lean back into paddling. My arms feel the pull of the water, and I fill my body with the sensation. Alec seems to get that the topic isn't my favorite, because he doesn't push; everyone at school knows what happened to my mom. Instead, as he paddles, he shifts to a new subject.

"How long have you played guitar?"

"Since before I can remember. Dad got me a ukulele when I was tiny — not the guitar I wanted so badly — because a ukulele is smaller, easier to start with. But tell me about you. I mean, stuff I don't know from class."

"What do you know from class?"

I lift my oar and turn back to him. Boy, he's cute when he looks at me like that. I say, "Um, you've been living in Edenville as long as me. Like, forever. You live with your parents. You work at Eb's Outdoors. You aren't good at math. You are super-good at history."

"I am, too, good at math."

"Whatever." Smiling, I tilt my face up to the sun. It means I'm not looking when Alec stands. The canoe lurching makes me grab the sides. "What are you doing?"

"Feel like a swim?"

"Sure. But I don't have a swimsuit."

"Neither do I." His eyes are alight.

"Ah. The amazing thing you promised," I say, deadpan. "Alec Sandcross gets naked and goes for a swim."

"No, that's not it."

He pulls off his shirt. My eyes travel over his tanned, muscular arms and six-pack.

"There maybe isn't anything amazing ..."

I splash water at him. "You lied to stop me writing. I thought that might be the deal."

The canoe tips but rights itself as I wobble to my feet.

"Okay then, the amazing thing ... is that you're going to take your clothes off, too," he says.

I unzip my life jacket. I hesitate and check around. The Fields family can't be seen, and the water is glassy quiet. Alec smiles his lazy smile. Then I do it. I pull off my shirt. Thank God I'm wearing a decent bra.

We're faltering and goofing off, and then suddenly we're giggling as he crouches and tugs off his jeans and I do the same — tricky in a canoe. We're stripped down to our underwear. The sun is amazing-warm against my skin. He steps closer along the canoe, causing it to tip again. I bet he's gonna come up to me and kiss me.

Instead he turns to the water. "Come on."

A shout stops us. "Help! Oh, my God, someone help me!"

It's Suzanne. I thought we were far from everyone, but I catch sight of her flailing in the water just through the reeds.

And I glimpse a red life jacket.

Annabelle!

She's floating facedown on the other side of the canoe from Suzanne. Alec and I glance at each other. Alec dives, and I jump. The water is as cold as death. I lift my face to orient myself, pushing hair out of my eyes, and then, focused, I knife through the water.

Now Annabelle is about ten yards away from me. Suzanne is still flailing in the reeds.

"Help her!"

Just then Alec cries out. I glance back. He's about ten yards behind me, *blood* pouring from his temple. His eyes are glassy.

"I banged my ... I ..."

He's sinking. "Alec!"

"I can't get to her!" Suzanne fights the reeds that have entangled her.

I turn back. I'm halfway between Annabelle and Alec. I have to save them. Alec is going under. Annabelle is facedown. I can't breathe. Pain radiates through my chest. I tread water, frantically looking one way and then the other.

I do not know who to choose.

Suzanne screams, "Lark! DO SOMETHING!"

But I *can't.*

I'm shattered glass
Shatter me, me, me
A moment in pieces
Take a shard of me
Look deeply inside for remnants
Of how we used to be
Part the water, slide in a ripple
Find yourself in time
Find me.
Parallel you, parallel me.

Chapter One
Chapter One

Day 1: early

My stomach hurts, and my eyes ache. I haven't slept. I sit on the front step, holding my coffee cup tightly. Tangled branches overhang our yard. It's not even nine in the morning, but the heat is rising already. I'm listening to St. Vincent while I watch Dad pick tomatoes. Even from here, their leaves smell rich and dense, almost spicy. Because he's a mechanic, he has grease on his shirt from work, but it hasn't stopped him wearing it again.

Alec's truck arrives. I remove one earbud and watch him get out. He's wearing his usual outdoorsy clothes, and he's holding three red roses. Roses again. I think of the orange ones that I left in his truck yesterday. I wonder if he threw them out after what happened. Alec steps through our gate, seeming giant in our nineteenth-century English garden–style yard, his shoes crunching on the gravel path, and he holds out the bouquet to me. My eyes travel over him. The neat stitches are stark against the skin of his temple. His shirt is pale green, and his hoodie is emblazoned with the slogan HIT THE WOODS. His sleeves are pushed back, revealing his strong, tanned arms. The air stills, and a bird calls a warning overhead. *I chose him, I chose him, I chose him.* I left a little girl facedown in the water. The bird calls again, and it sounds to me like a judgment. I swallow my nausea, seeking Alec's gaze to reassure me I made the right choice. I catch his eye. Something between us quickens, intensifies, becomes solid.

"You look ..." He pauses, as if he's finding the right word, his tongue resting on the right of his bottom lip, close to his piercing. "Lovely."

"I look tired." I smile wanly. I take the roses. "Thanks."

"I didn't sleep either." He turns to my dad, who has emerged from the bushes. "Mr. Hardy? A pleasure to meet you." He even reaches out to shake Dad's hand. "I mean, I know we saw each other yesterday."

He means at the hospital, where Dad had to come and get me. Where Alec had to be checked over. Where little Annabelle is in a coma.

Suzanne asked us not to visit her. "Family only, please," she said. Not unkindly, but with a quiet firmness.

Alec continues. "But that feels like months ago ..."

"Call me 'Vince.' 'Mr. Hardy' makes me feel old."

"Will do. Thank you, Vince." Alec turns to me. "I just wanted to check you were okay."

I tremble. I can still hear that desperate cry: *Lark! DO SOMETHING!*

Day 3: period three

Alec's thumb circles my palm, and shivers spread through me. I could write about this feeling, put it in a song. I think about the last time I wrote a song and push away the lyrics that are trying to come. Instead I peek at his hand, his silver thumb ring, his bitten nails. He's wearing one of those checkered shirts that make him look like he's on his way to hike up a mountain. His jeans have that rugged look, too — not skinny or trendy. The "man outside" look works for me. Yep. Works for me. The piercing in the middle of his bottom lip doesn't quite fit the look, but I like it, too. I look everywhere but at the stitches on his temple. They only remind me of what I did. His clothes contrast totally with what I'm wearing: a black shirt, short black skirt and knee-high low-heeled boots.

It's the first day back at school after the summer break, and it's already the period before lunch. The day has gone by without me really being a part of it. Mr. Hidlebaugh, tall, bald and enthusiastic, stands at the front of the class emphatically talking about *The Road* by Cormac McCarthy. His hands make huge gestures, and then he writes *Who is anyone really?* on the smartboard.

But I hardly pay attention. The world has tilted on its axis. My mind clutters with images of Annabelle in the water. She was dusky blue. My heart pounds. I have to get out of here. Suzanne's shriek echoes in my head. Alec's thumb tracks another slow circle, and I take a breath. Cool it. I hear my cell, but no message appears. I silence it.

"The boy is asking who the footprints belong to," Hidlebaugh cries. He raises his right arm and brings it down in a chopping motion. "Who? I ask you."

We're sitting at desks in a U shape. Alec is on one side of me, Lucy the other. I lean my shoulder against hers. She smells of the horrible clove cigarettes she always smokes, and of incense. The incense gets in her strawberry-blond hair at her mom's store. Her mom, Dolphin — her actual name — was my mom's best friend. Lucy pushes her shoulder against mine.

Finally, finally, the bell rings. We only have a half day the first day, so school is over.

Alec is still holding my hand as we file out into the crowded hallway of Edenville High. Lucy asks if we want to go for lunch.

I glance at Alec, who is staring into space, not really listening. "You know what, Luce?" I say. "Why don't I call you later."

She flashes me a smile. "Sure."

We've known each other since we were babies, so I know she means *Go for it, Lark. Have fun with the new guy.*

"See ya later, lovebirds."

Alec slips his hand from mine and rests it around my waist. My whole body feels his heat.

We walk across the parking lot away from the school. The day is so soft, so luminously agreeable, that my skin becomes part of the weather. My mood suddenly brightens, and my thoughts float across my mind as lightly as the shining white clouds above. Alec tightens his grip around my waist, pulling me slightly toward him. I stumble. He catches hold of me, and we end up facing each other.

"You trying to make me fall?" I say. It's corny, but I don't care.

"Mebbe."

I glance at his mouth, the piercing there. If he kissed me, would I feel the metal in his lip? Electricity sparks between us.

"You hungry?" he says.

"Sure. What do you want?" I ask, then blush at my accidental innuendo. "I mean … to eat. How about a burger?"

"Burger! Lark — the Chicken Shack is the way to go. I'll convert you."

"To greasy, triple-fried wings? I don't think so."

"I'm pretty persuasive. But first, sing me something." He tugs my hand and steps back from me.

"Sing?" I glance around the parking lot. "You don't mean here."

"Why not?"

"I — I haven't really got anything new right now."

"An old song, then."

"I don't have my guitar."

"Guitar? Do you need it with you to sing?"

"Honestly? No." I watch other kids get into their cars or wander to the usual lunch places. "Anyway, I don't use that guitar anymore."

"Why?"

"Uh, next question, please …"

"Interesting." He taps his chin like he's pretending to be working something out. "Ms. Lark has a secret. I'll get it out of her. But not before I've heard her sing."

"I won't! You can't make me!" I say, dramatically stepping back.

He narrows his eyes. "So-o-o-o, what type of guitar is it? This one you don't use?"

"You won't get my secrets from me." I smile at him coyly.

"But I will answer you that. The one I actually use belonged to Iona, but I also have a Takamine guitar. A Tak — that's what it's called in the business. It's an electric acoustic." I remember the feel of it. "It has a pickup built into it for amplification."

"What's that?"

"A pickup? It's a small electronic device, set right into the body of the guitar, that picks up the sound."

"But you don't use it. And you don't have Iona's guitar here. So … there's just you, me and your voice." He produces a pair of sunglasses from his shirt pocket. "You can pretend I'm not looking. Sing!"

"It's not that I'm worried about you looking." I'm not sure how such an innocent statement comes out sounding so dirty. "Okay." I hold up my hands. "Okay. I'll do it." I glance once more around the emptying parking lot and start to sing:

"We were this close to the water
My hair in my eyes
And the sun
High above us
When you told me it was done
Since then I've been running
Oh, you make me run
To get back to the moment
When you told me I'm the one."

A couple of kids stop walking and clap. I shut up. What am I doing? I just sang in the parking lot. "So yeah. It's been on my mind. I wrote it long before … before. But it changes the whole meaning."

Alec takes two steps to be next to me again and pulls me close. He lifts his sunglasses, and the electricity between us surges again. He drops his mouth to mine. His kiss is quick and gentle, and his lips taste of sunshine and honey. My whole body turns molten. He pulls his mouth away to look at me, and in his dark eyes I see a glint of light. My mouth follows his, and we kiss again. He slides his hand into my hair, and hot sparks shoot down my neck and spine.

I hear Lucy yell, "Classy, Lark." I give her the finger while we keep kissing.

Alec surfaces first and tugs me toward the Chicken Shack, where we order a huge tub of wings. They smell greasy and delicious, and they are. We sit on bar stools in the window, time passing like there is no such thing as time at all. We listen to a singer I've just discovered — Tei Shi. One earbud each. We talk about music, about hiking, about a band I want to go and see, about climbing, about everything and nothing. He looks at me while I wipe chicken grease off my mouth. Sure, not the most romantic moment in history, but as his eyes meet mine, I have the feeling that I know Alec. I shudder in a good way. He feels familiar, like we've met before, like we're connected, like … like he's my soul mate. Who knew I even believed in soul mates? But suddenly it seems blazingly obvious that of course we each have a soul mate, and there, with fried chicken on my lips, I find the person who might be mine.

Alec has to run an errand, so he can't drop me home. After we kiss goodbye, I float onto the bus, drift into my seat, yawn and check my cell. Alec has sent a photo of the climbing wall downtown.

Alec:

Wanna join me there Saturday?

Lark:

Am working —

how about Sunday?

Alec:

Blow off work.

Lark:

Can't!

Alec:

Sunday then.

See you tomorrow.

Lark:

After band practice.

We always practice on Sunday.

Alec:

You playing hard to get? xxx

My heart quickens at the xxx sign-off. What is with me? Even superhot-and-heavy Jared didn't turn me to jelly like this. I daydream against the seat, watching as we cross over the main bridge but averting my eyes from the swift river below. It burns in my mind, and as I close my eyes, I see the lake, the water, Annabelle. I get out at the bus stop a few blocks from my house, deciding to walk in the sunshine to clear the images. Quickly the warmth of the day improves my mood, and I arrive home, humming the song I sang to Alec, to find my dad tending his flower garden. We live in a small clapboard house built in 1912, the year Edenville became a city.

"Someone's happier," Dad says, brushing his hands against his shirt.

"Yeah. Things with Alec are … they're maybe … good."

Dad plucks a dead flower head from the bush.

Suzanne:
Thanks for your message, Lark.
No change here.
I'll let you know when you can visit.

In a heartbeat, the bright day dissipates. I can't believe I've been smiling while Annabelle is in the hospital. I remember her slack face, damp lashes, the shrill of the ambulance siren.

"At least no change means she's not worse," I say to Dad.

"Lark, you know you did everything you could, right?"

"If only I'd … I took too long …" Tears spring to my eyes, and though Dad tries to comfort me, I just want to forget about what happened, so I head into the house to start supper.

I cut onions and fry them in butter, then add a little flour, stock and milk to make gravy, which is how Mom used to do it. I place four sausages into a pan with a bit of maple syrup and water, cover the whole thing with foil and put it in the oven to bake. I watch some reality crap on TV and then boil water to make pasta. Then I prep a simple salad and lay two plates and cutlery on the table.

When everything's ready, I go outside to find Dad, who's talking to Cayson "Nifty" Nifteneger. Nifty is tall and insanely skinny. He and Iona used to compete to see who was going to be the tallest, but Nifty won by three inches. He's into clothes and music, and right now he's dressed like we're living in New York, with his hair spiked and a fashionably cut tee that falls loosely around his shoulders.

"Hey, wildcat," Nifty says, slipping his e-cig into his shirt pocket. "You coming to band practice?"

"'Course."

Dad nods at us before disappearing inside.

"How was your day?" I ask Nifty.

"Same old." He works at a music store full-time since he dropped out of high school last year. "Got anything new for us?"

I think about the song I sang to Alec. It's one the band has never heard. My stomach twists at the thought of sharing it or the other song I started on my birthday, so I reply, "Not today."

"Okay, soon, though. We gotta get ready for the show."

"Show?"

"Hell, yes. We're on at Lydia's. I'm pretty sure we are, anyway. Hey, I hear you're dating that sexy-hot ninja hunk," he says.

"Ninja?"

"The parkour guy — right? Alec Sandcross. Wild and crazy stuntman."

"I don't know that we're *dating.*"

"Mmm-hmm." He swivels his hips. "That's my Lark, baby." He pauses. "How's the little girl?"

"Same." I flash back to Annabelle being lifted limply from the water.

"You okay?"

"I'm okay if I don't think about it. Wanna join us for supper?"

Nifty shakes his head and gets on his bike. "Nah, I'm going for a ride. But I do need a little advice about something."

Alec:

Just thinking about you.

Lark:

Good.

"Bye, then, La-aa-aark," Nifty sings.

I glance up from my phone and smile. I can't stop smiling. "Sorry, you wanted some advice?"

"I gotta go now."

"See you later, at practice," I call.

He pretends to tip an imaginary cap before he pedals away.

Day 7: Sunday afternoon

Iona's parents are über rich. Their garage alone is bigger than the main floor of my house. Every Wednesday and Sunday, our band meets here. Her parents have cleared out the back half of the garage, and Iona has her drum kit here and a bunch of equipment. My favorite spot is the old blue three-person couch, where I'm sitting this Sunday, playing with the jewel on my belly chain, which dangles out over my jeans. When Iona has parties in this garage, I people-watch from this spot. It's a great way to get ideas for songs. Suddenly I have an overpowering feeling of déjà vu. It makes me so dizzy I lean my head over my knees. The weird feeling quickly passes. I probably need something to eat.

Alec:
Not long now.

Lark:
Too long.

I look over at the rest of the band — Iona, Nifty, Reid. We've been playing together since we were fourteen — after my mom died — but we haven't got a name right now. We were the Specials Board for a while, and for at least five months before that, Nifty convinced us that Glass Returns was a good name, and before that I think we were Goodly Animals. On Wednesday after school we talked it over again, but Nifty, Iona and Reid all vetoed the name I suggested: Exploding Night of the Zesty Solitude. I told them I got it off an internet band-name generator. It was ironic cool. They weren't convinced.

Nifty is noodling on his guitar and chatting to Reid, who is sitting at his keyboard and trying out a melody that Nifty wants him to work on. Iona is tapping her bass drum with one foot and messaging on her cell. I remember fighting with Iona for the dress-up clothes at preschool and throwing sand at Nifty. Iona was a total princess as a little kid. Now she's just under six feet tall, with huge dark bangs, crazy wild makeup all the time. Today she's drawn a blue-and-yellow star over one eye, Roller Derby–style. She's been getting more into Roller Derby recently and often heads out after practice on Sundays for a couple of hours at the rink. She's wearing a black leather jacket with US flags sewn all over it and a corset underneath that shows off her super curves. She volunteers at the crisis nursery, and the little kids think she's the coolest girl in the world.

I wonder if we'd all have ended up friends if we hadn't been in preschool together. We're into different crowds now at school. Reid's a techie, loves reading HTML and is hell-bent on being some geek superstar. He has square glasses, green eyes — his eyes are vivid, a contrast against his dark hair and sideburns. His parents fled the Iraq War and came here to Edenville. He's never talked about it in all the years we've known each other. Iona's a third-wave girl, furiously fighting for women's rights. Nifty, who was the year above us, hung with the hipsters — although he hates the term — before he dropped out of school. Since meeting Cole, he's regretted dropping out.

I cozy back up on the couch and read over the messages Alec has already sent me today. This whole week at school, things have been building up between us. Kisses against the gym wall.

Hand holding at lunch. Long conversations in his pickup when he drives me home, then sitting in the truck for ages outside my house. As I read, he messages again:

Alec:
You ready?
Finished work early.

Our Sunday practice has been kinda flat. I haven't really gotten off the couch or warmed up my voice, and it doesn't help that Nifty's in the worst mood.

Lucy:
Climbing?
He's totally going to check out your butt!

Lark:
I know. Urgh.
Am wearing skinny jeans.
Right choice?

Lucy:
Hahahaha!

Nifty interrupts. "Lark, he-ll-o-o-o-o. I told you there's a chance of a show at Lydia's in October. We need to focus."

"We'll be fine," I say. "You worry too much. And the show's not even a sure thing, right? Maybe we should just quit today. You're not in the mood."

"You're the one who's not in the mood." Nifty scowls at me,

pulls his e-cig from his pocket and then puts it back again.

Alec:
We on?

Lark:
Definitely on — coming now.
We're done here.

"Ooooh, lovergirl," Iona sings, distracting me.

I throw a balled-up paper bag from the brownie I bought at D'Lish and read Alec's next message:

Alec:
Am here. Came to watch.
But even better.

My heart jumps as Alec arrives at the garage door, ignoring my bandmates' eye rolling. I go to him, and he puts his arms around me, bending to kiss me, briefly. I feel the metal of his stud hard inside his lip. Just having him close makes me feel safe, comforted, like I can do anything. Iona wolf-whistles.

Alec pulls away and says to the others, "Thought I'd get my girl."

As I grab my longboard and the rest of my stuff, tingling from being called his "girl," even though it's sappy, I catch Reid's eyes. They cloud with an unreadable emotion before he pulls his cell from his pocket and stares at it.

I swing Alec's hand. "You know everyone, right?"

Alec nods. He's never hung out with any of the band, but

everyone knows everyone at Edenville High. He takes my board as we walk out into the cool fall afternoon. "Wanna try free climbing instead of the wall?" he asks.

"I heard you were into that." The wind blows, and I nestle into my jacket. I found it at a thrift store, and it's silver-gray, down to my thighs.

"Who from?"

"Nifty says you're into wild and crazy stunts."

"Yeah, like what?"

"Apparently you're an urban ninja."

"Oooh," he says, dropping my board and jumping on. "I like that." He directs the board toward the curb and flips it fully before landing back on it. "I can be an urban ninja."

"How did you get into it?"

"Parkour is used a lot in video games. The designers motion-capture people for the games by filming parkour. The way that heroes move — well, I gamed enough, saw parkour enough, I wanted to try it. I loved it. It makes me feel … free." His expression momentarily darkens.

A loud motorbike roars by as Alec nimbly leaps onto a wall, leaving my board on the ground. He somersaults to one side and lands on a small, squat brick structure I hadn't even noticed.

"Sweet." A few leaves fall in swirling patterns, and new lyrics come to me: It makes me feel … free.

"That's called a 'precision drop' — when you have a long surface that isn't wide." He jumps lightly to the ground next to me. "You don't move when you land."

"You make it look easy!"

"It gets easier the more you do it. Try it." He spins around, his arms out wide, and tilts back to look at the sky. "Here

I am, free as a bird, trying to convince my girl to give it a whirl." He stops to look at me. "Maybe I should leave the songwriting to you."

"No, that was pretty good. At least the lines rhymed." I laugh. "But I don't need convincing. I'll try it. What do you want to free-climb?"

"How about the old hotel? We'd have to wait until closer to twilight. A couple of hours. Then we'd be fine. We'll get the elevator up to the eighth floor. I've done it before. There's a window. I'll show you."

"The eighth floor? That sounds ... high."

"We can practice stuff until then."

His words tug at my mind. *Twilight. The eighth floor. I've done it before.* A couple of notes play around with the lyrics in my head, tumbling over each other like autumn leaves. I pull out my cell to make notes. There's a message:

Alec not surfacing,
the reflection in the water
of the sky above.

There's no number. The message vanishes, but my head begins to pound.

"What's up?" Alec gently touches my cheek.

"Just my cell. I got a weird ..." I move back from him and rub my temples. "It was really ... I don't even know." I check my cell again. There's no message. "Let's go."

By the time we've driven downtown and walked along the river for a while, practicing a few wall climbs and jumps, it's late afternoon. We buy take-out coffees and sit on a bench with our hands wrapped around the warm disposable cups, occasionally looking up at the hotel. I pull out my phone and put in one earbud, giving Alec the other. Together we listen to Alvvays. The vocalist's voice is high, subtle, nuanced, and I love it. After two songs, Alec takes out the earbud.

"You don't like it?" I hold my hand to my chest.

"Well, it's maybe … uh … maybe just a bit girlie."

"Girlie? She's got great lyrics. A gorgeous voice."

"Okay, sure. She's not all high-pitched and emotional."

I jab him in the ribs. "You're a sexist monster."

"I'm a sexy what?"

"A sexist —"

He presses his mouth to mine. When we come up for air, he grins and says, "Can we climb now?"

At the hotel, a tall, thin guy opens the front door for us. A memory trickles into my mind. My mom and I came here, to this hotel lobby, and we sat here. I must have been nine. We drank hot chocolate and pretended to be rich and famous. At one point she sat at the piano. That one, right there. She began to play, and the other people sitting around stopped what they were doing to listen. And then, just as I'm trying to remember the exact sound of her voice, the memory is gone. There is only the shiny hotel lobby, the burble of other guests, and Muzak, bringing me back to the present.

Alec is saying, "It's about having three points of contact at all times."

"What is?"

"Climbing. I was just telling you. I'm guessing you weren't listening."

"Sorry. I was just …"

He moves his thumb lightly over my cheek, then rests it on my bottom lip. "Ready now for a climbing lesson?"

I kiss his thumb and nod. The elevator doors squeak closed; the motor whirs as it goes up. We're reflected in the glass.

"Three points of contact. One hand two feet, or two hands one foot. But this isn't hard climbing. Not at all — the pitch of the roof up there isn't steep. We can take some pictures, watch the sunset. Ready?"

I nod. My stomach has a stone in it.

He takes my hand and says, "Nervous?"

"Not really." My fingers lace with his. "Yeah. Totally nervous."

My heart races as he kisses me. His tongue is rough, and his hand slides over my shirt, then underneath it to graze my belly button, then slowly upward. My body responds, and I hear a groan escape my lips as he kisses my collarbone. A shiver runs along my arms.

The elevator dings. Alec steps back as the door whines open. I feel keenly the space where he was moments before. I want him to kiss me like that again. I wonder if it's because I chose him that my feelings are so intense. Or the opposite. I chose him over Annabelle because this boy is the one. Urgh. I didn't know I could be so mushy. Just as well I haven't written any songs for a few days; they'd be schlock.

He pulls me into a carpeted hallway, where there's a faint musty smell. At the end of the corridor is a window looking over the dusky sky. The setting sun is huge and orange. Alec draws a screwdriver from his pocket.

"Always handy?" I joke.

"Yeah. Moments like this. Keep watch for me?"

I look over my shoulder, but no one's up here. I imagine a

security guy viewing us on a monitor somewhere, getting up, coming to stop us, but I hear only the hum of the fluorescent lights and the chime of the elevator, now on a distant floor.

When I turn back, the window is open, and Alec is standing on the window ledge. "Ready?" he says.

My cell vibrates.

Dad:
What's for supper?
Kidding — but where are you?
Eating cheese sandwich.

Lark:
Out with Alec.
Back soon. LU.

A new message appears, no number:

He strikes a pose
as if he's on the cover of Vogue ...

"Alec?" I say.

He's not at the window. I hurry to look out. He's standing to my right on a narrow ledge — maybe six inches wide — that juts from the wall and is decorated with gargoyles. The cool evening air is like a drink of water.

"It's beautiful out here," he says.

I glance at my cell. The message is gone. This is weird.

"Come on, Lark."

I put away my phone and pull myself out of the window,

my stomach tight as a perfect lyric. *Boom* — racing heart, hot cheeks, eight stories to the ground below, Alec Sandcross poised on the ledge. He shuffles a few steps, and so I do, too, not looking down, my back pressed against the rough stucco. Then he steps up onto a higher narrow ledge, and I follow. He turns to face the wall, reaches up one arm, loose limbed as a chimpanzee, and pulls himself up and over the overhang. Everything is quiet and still. I hear a bump and scrape, and then both his hands appear, followed by his face.

"Let me get you over this bit."

I hesitate. But there's no way I can pull myself up like he did without help.

"I won't let you go," he says.

"Holy crap, this is scary." I half turn on the ledge and stretch out one of my hands to his. His grip is strong. I grab his other hand, my body stiffening with the thought that if he lets go, I'll die.

"Relax, Lark."

Then everything happens quickly. He pulls, while I scrabble for a foothold, terror lurching in my heart like a drunk. My legs freewheel, but his grip is strong, and he easily tugs me over onto the roof. I scrape the skin on my stomach, and my belly chain snaps off, slipping over the edge, but I don't care. The roof tiles are large, but the pitch isn't steep, as he said, and from here, the rising moon hangs just out of grasp. From here, it's more a matter of crawling upward than climbing to get to the top, and I'm trembling all over, refusing to look down, until we straddle the peak and sit facing each other. We did it.

After my breathing steadies, I look down. Another pulse of excitement shoots through me — below, the city spreads out like a fabric patterned with buildings, cars, tiny people, and I am here, invisible, watching, flying above the city, adrenaline hot in my veins.

"Woo-hoo!" I cry.

"Told you," Alec says.

He kisses me hard, his tongue warm and wet, and our knees press together. Something shoots through me — I haven't felt like this before. God, I want him to kiss me more, kiss me harder. I become liquid. I don't want to name this feeling, but the L-word floats through my mind, springs to my lips, which open more. Nothing has felt like this before. Nothing like Alec.

Nothing like this.

Day 13: late afternoon

The river glitters between the thick trees on its banks. Alec pulls down the blind and lightly pushes me onto the dark-gray cover of his tidy bed. It smells freshly laundered, but with a not-unpleasant undertone of sweat. St.Vincent — my choice — starts on "I Prefer Your Love." I sit up to wriggle out of my jeans and throw them onto the spotless floor. Alec kneels at the edge of the bed and pulls his shirt over his head. His toned abs flex as he leans forward to kiss the point of my chin, then the place where my collarbones meet, then the top of my breasts. I bite my lip, and a sigh involuntarily escapes me. I turn my head. Posters of scantily clad female climbers adorn the dark-blue walls. A map of the world is lacquered onto his desk, and books line the shelves. The desk has a large computer and a laptop.

My hands play with his hair, and I say, my voice husky, "Are you sure your parents aren't coming home?"

He props himself on his forearms. "They said they'd be out all day." Quietly he adds, "You're beautiful, Lark. And I love your name."

The word *love* hums between us. Again. But it's way too soon. He leans over me and strokes my hair, looking into my eyes, and the feeling buds in me again.

"Tell me — have you, you know, a lot?" I ask.

Amusement glimmers in his eyes. "Have I … you know? What would you mean by that?"

"Come on," I say.

"Why?"

"I dunno. Curious." I blush. "Not my business."

"Your business. A few others. Only one who — I guess that meant anything."

"Who was that?"

His face clouds. "Sharbat, from school."

"Yeah, I knew you guys dated."

He draws a mountain range over my chest with one finger.

"Her parents didn't want us to be together — they're pretty old-fashioned. They broke us up. They made her leave the school. It was ... it was pretty bad. But I'm over it now. And it's led to good things ... like you."

He kisses my shoulder.

"And that's when I really got into climbing. Which gave me a huge new focus. I want to travel, see the world ... climb this." He points at one of the posters of rock faces. "I mean, it would be awesome to be able to do that one day."

The front door slams. Alec turns off the music, and we both start hopping around the bedroom, grabbing our clothes.

I hear a woman whimper, "Please don't."

"Wait here," Alec says. He zips up his jeans, yanks his shirt over his head and rushes out of the room and down the stairs.

He isn't quick enough to stop me overhearing a man shouting — like, really yelling — "What the hell, Karen?"

I get my shirt on as Alec says loudly, "Lark's here."

Alec's dad clears his throat. "We'll talk later," he says, plainly at Alec's mom.

I check my makeup in my compact and smooth my hair — in the semidarkness of Alec's room, my hair seems even blacker than usual. When I come out of the bedroom, I try to act normal. Like I'm not coming out of Alec's bedroom. Like hearing Alec's dad shouting isn't awkward.

Alec's parents stand by the front door, looking up at me as I come down the stairs. His mom is tall and slim. She wears amazingly high heels, skinny jeans and a white cashmere sweater. Her blond hair is immaculate, and her golden gel nails gleam. From her flawlessly made-up face, her very pale eyes assess me.

She smiles and air-kisses my cheeks. "Hi, Lark, a pleasure."

Alec's dad is hugely tall and built like a garden shed — boxy. He wears a gray suit and a navy tie. His dark eyes are the same as Alec's. He's clean-shaven, with close-cropped hair.

He puts a hand forward for me to shake and says, "You are just as beautiful as Alec said." His voice is jovial and friendly. "Call me 'Scott.'"

My hand seems tiny held in his. He has a gold ring on his little finger. The spicy smell of his cologne wafts over me.

"Um, thanks," I say, as he releases me. "Nice to meet you both. I should probably go, though. I'm supposed to be working in — oh, uh — ten minutes ago."

"Where do you work?" Scott asks.

"D'Lish over on Temperance. It's close to my house. Great coffee."

"Well, come by again sometime, Lark. Have supper with us — right, Karen?" He turns to Alec's mom.

She says, "Absolutely. Alec has been talking about you."

I would be thrilled if it wasn't all so … tense between everyone.

Alec doesn't meet my eye; he just mumbles a goodbye. As soon as the door shuts behind me, he messages:

Alec:
Sorry. Meet after ur done work?

Lark:

Course xox

I grab my longboard from the front porch. I'm wearing clothes for a warm day, but it's surprisingly cool. I'm pulling on a hoodie when I hear Scott yell, really yell, "I saw that girl come out of your room! I'm no idiot."

"Not now, Dad."

"Who do the pair of you think you are?"

I'm late for work. I shouldn't be listening at closed doors. I swallow hard and then scoot away.

Lucy gives me a dirty look when I get to D'Lish, where the tables are stacked with cups and plates, and there's a long lineup. People sit eating desserts, chatting, checking their cells. The low evening lighting illuminates the series of photographs of the river that has just been hung. I clear tables, while Lucy deals with the customers. The whole shift is crazy, and it's not until after we've put the Closed sign on the door and said goodnight to the last customer that I even get a chance to apologize for not being on time.

The beads on her multicolored bandanna jangle as she shakes her head. "I'm gonna take a five-minute break."

"I'm sorry. Really."

"You've been late three times working with me in the past week. But that was crazy late. Let me guess — you were with Alec." She holds her hands together, fingers pressed, and lets out a slow breath. "Give me five minutes. I'm exhausted. It's been so-o-o-o busy." She opens the oven and takes out the breakfast muffins for the morning, filling the back kitchen with the warm smell of bananas and toasted oats. "It's not a big deal. I'm obviously just jealous I'm not getting it."

"But I am sorry. And I'm not getting it." I grin at her. "Yet."

Lucy leans against the counter and her eyebrows dance. "O-o-o-oh!" She opens her pack of cigarettes. Even though she hasn't yet lit one, the strong clove smell drifts over.

"It's not just that," I say, and she giggles. "I mean … he's so … he wants to do all this stuff, like travel and climb famous rocks. I just … what am I trying to say … I guess …"

"Are you in love?" She giggles again. "You're utterly in love. I haven't seen you like this."

I beam. "And he's hot. So freaking hot."

"That is very true."

"Go smoke. I'll clear up in here."

"One thing, Gooey-ball … try not to get so distracted by Alec you forget about the rest of us. Okay?"

"As if I would."

She pops the end of a cigarette into her mouth. "When I get back, tell me more about you nearly getting it."

She goes out, and I place the muffins on a rack to cool. I put dishes and pots in the dishwasher and run hot water to start wiping the countertops. A weird feeling that I can't shake rises through me. I'm a little unstable, a little dizzy. Figuring I'm hungry, I grab myself a cookie, but it doesn't improve anything. I've got Anika, Boh and Hollie playing on my cell, and normally "Peace of Mind" makes me feel calmer, but I'm jittery, my mind filling with images of the lake on that day. The weight of Alec as I kicked to the shore. The wet, snaking reeds. Annabelle's blue lips.

While I clean up, I dial the hospital. I've called two other times recently, but Reception in Pediatrics kept telling me the family isn't taking any calls, and Suzanne hasn't answered her cell.

A woman picks up on the first ring, sounding monumentally bored. "St. Mary's. How may I direct your call?"

"I, um, I want to come visit a patient. Her first name is Annabelle. Annabelle Fields. She's in a coma. She's a little kid —"

The woman cuts me off, and two seconds later the phone rings and is answered by a tired female voice: "Hello?"

"I hope I didn't disturb you. Sorry," I say.

"No. I wasn't asleep."

"Suzanne? It's Lark. Sorry. I'm really sorry — God, it's late," I babble. "I thought I'd get Pediatrics Reception."

"No. It's sweet of you to call. I wish I had better news. There's no … there's no change. Oh …" A sob travels through the cell. "I find it hard to sleep. Just in case she wakes … I want my face to be the face she sees."

"Maybe I could help. I could come by later this week and watch her," I say. "With Alec, perhaps."

"Sure. Maybe."

Mechanically I wipe down the countertop. The silence stretches. "I'm sorry I dived for Alec first …" I blurt.

"Lark, there was nothing you could have done differently that day."

"I blame myself —"

She chokes back a sob. "Lark. Don't torture yourself. Anyone would have been dazed in that moment. You reacted in a perfectly normal way."

"But I could have moved more quickly, saved them both. I don't know —"

"If anything, I'm the one to blame."

We're both silent.

"Look, Lark, I need to sleep. But do come. If we're still here, come ... how about Tuesday? Okay?"

"Okay."

"Goodnight, honey." She ends the call.

Lucy comes in. "Thanks for clearing up."

During the call, I did more than I realized, so we're nearly finished for the night. Lucy gives me a hug, and the smell of clove curls off her clothes and hair.

She says, "I miss you, you know, now that you're all loved up. But I'm happy if you're happy."

"I *am* happy."

"Maybe Alec wants to come with us tonight? I wanna get to know him better. This guy who gets you loved up."

"Tonight?" I ask.

"Nitrogen Vice? At Lydia's?"

"Oh, yeah."

"You forgot?"

"No. 'Course not. I'll ask him right now."

I slot away a cookie sheet. Together we wrap the muffins. I message Alec. He messages back when Lucy and I are outside D'Lish, locking up:

Alec:

Can we meet alone instead?

Lark:

I promised Lucy.

Not that I remembered.

Alec:

Can you un-promise?

We need to talk.

My heart sputters. What does that mean?

Lark:

Where do you want to meet?

Should I be worried?

Alec:

When I say talk, I might mean something else … ;-)

Meet u at the play park by my house?

Lark:

Okay. Lucy will get over it.

Something else sounds good …

really good …

Lucy elbows my arm. "Is he going to meet us?"

"Would you mind if I bail?"

She rolls her eyes. "Would you mind if I mind?"

"Of course I'd mind! I can see Alec tomorrow. Let's go see the band. You and me."

She elbows me again. "No. Don't worry about it. Go. Get some."

She pulls out a clove cigarette. "Who am I to stand in the path of true love?"

"It's not love. And I'm not getting some."

"Yeah, you tell yourself that." She lights her cigarette. "'Alec and Lark, sitting in a tree. K-I-S-S-I-N-G.'"

I giggle. "Maybe it's a bit love. Thanks, Luce. See you later."

I hum a few bars of a possible song to myself as I put in my earbuds, and then I longboard away from Lucy in the bright moonlight toward the play park, where Alec is waiting for me.

Day 16: afternoon

After school on Tuesday, Alec drives us over to the hospital. We get out in the parking lot, and I am taken back to the last time I was here. Three years ago Dad walked me to the car. As he opened the passenger door, I turned to look up at the blank windows, wondering what would happen to Mom's body. Loss grabs my heart and clenches it.

Alec says, "Hey, Planet Lark, all okay?"

I nod minutely.

He takes my hand and interlaces his fingers with mine. We figure our way through the warren of hospital rooms and find Annabelle's ward. When Suzanne opens Annabelle's door, she manages a wan smile.

"I was hoping we'd be out of here before now," she says.

Annabelle's blond hair spreads out in damp tendrils on the pillow. There is a red blotch on her left cheek.

Her mom brushes that cheek and says, "Did you know that patients in comas often end up the victims of medical errors? Annabelle's allergic to lanolin. I told them."

She slumps in an armchair and gestures for me to sit on the only other chair. Alec stands awkwardly by a cabinet on which several vases of wilted flowers are parked. Suzanne falls silent.

I put my hand softly on Annabelle's — it is so small and warm beneath mine. And so very still. The only sound is the soft in-and-out takes of her breath. Her eyes seem to be moving beneath her closed lids. As I watch, a tiny tear appears at the corner of her right eye. It slides down her cheek and slips onto the white bedsheet, where it leaves a watermark. The watermark begins spreading, as if more water were coming from somewhere. The color of the water darkens, browning.

I sense a static, a shimmer in the air. I glance up and see my *bedroom*, notes for a song scattered on my desk.

I gasp and let go of Annabelle's hand. What's happening?

Alec touches my shoulder. "You okay?"

"Um ..." Everything is as it was. I touch the bedsheet. It's dry. "I'm fine," I say. "Yeah. Just ..." I catch Suzanne's gaze. "I'm sorry," I say.

Chapter Two

Chapter Two

Day 1: early

Tangled branches overhang our yard. It's not even nine in the morning, but the heat is rising already. I'm listening to St. Vincent while Dad picks tomatoes. Their leaves smell rich and dense, almost spicy. I flick through my cell to check, again, if there's been any update. Nothing.

"Do you think we can go now, Dad?"

"Of course. You ready?" He winces slightly and puts one hand to his chest.

"What's wrong?"

"I'm fine."

"Dad?"

"Just a twinge. It's nothing to worry about, remember?" He wipes his hands on his pants and pulls the car key from his pocket. "Let's go."

*

We sit at a traffic light, time slowing down. The song I was writing when I was in the truck with Alec — yesterday, a thousand years ago — plays in my mind. I swallow back nausea.

It was a total freak accident. Alec hit his head on a rock, which caused him to lose consciousness. Your head is, like, a danger zone. A six-year-old boy falls from a low wooden beam at the play park. Brain is damaged forever. A ten-year-old stumbles at the shopping mall. Is in a coma. For, like, *years*. A fifteen-year-old from a small town outside Edenville gets his four-wheeler stuck under a faulty garage door. The door crushes his head. Dead. Trust me. I've been Googling this crap all night. Who knew the fabric of life was so thin? Not Alec. If he'd dived half an inch to the right, half an inch to the left. If he hadn't hit his head at that exact spot, well, he might have been the one to save Annabelle. If I hadn't waited so long to make a choice. Then, if I'd swum to him instead of Annabelle, he might not have lost consciousness, swallowed so much water. He might just have had a headache. Or a bruise. Or nothing. Thinking that I might have saved him stirs memories of blood, of him sinking, but when I try to picture that moment, I'm dizzy. I hear screaming. Pain radiates through my chest.

Dad eases the car from one lane to another. "Did you call them?"

I shake my head and stare out the car window.

"Sweetheart, you should call before we show up. I know you're upset they haven't let you see him, but you have to call his family." Dad pulls the car over to the side of the road and gives me a look.

I get out my phone and press in Alec's home number, which I got from the class list.

A woman answers. I recognize her voice: it's Alec's mom, who I met briefly at the hospital yesterday.

"Hi, it's … it's Lark."

There's a long pause, so I wonder if she's still there. Then she says, "How can I help you? I'm only home to get a change of clothes. I'm on my way back. To the hospital."

"I'm sorry to bother you. I just wanted to know … how is he?"

"No change."

I can't stop tears. "Can I maybe … can I come and see him?"

"There's really no change." She falls silent. "Just family, Lark. We just need time."

I nod, although she can't see me, and tears slip down my cheeks.

Dad catches my look and swings the wheel to aim us toward home.

"Maybe tomorrow," Alec's mom says. "Maybe tomorrow."

Day 3: period three, almost

The first day of the school year, third period, and my classmates are heading into English with Mr. Hidlebaugh. A message pops onto my cell.

Alec's thumb circles my palm and shivers spread through me.

The message vanishes. I press the screen several times, my heart racing and my breathing fast: What does it mean? I can't find any record of it or the sender anywhere. I look up and realize I'm alone in the walkway; the bell has rung, my class has started, and I feel like I'm about to throw up.

I jam my cell into my pocket, my teeth chattering but not from cold, and I walk away. I have to get out of here. As I leave, the front doors of Edenville High swing shut behind me.

Our school is at the top of the only hill in the city. Edenville is one of the flattest cities in the world — a driver almost never has to use a hand brake. Not that I passed my driving test. I hurry away from the old building with its quirks, down the hill, past my bus stop. I check my phone for the bus times, but I've just missed one.

Far above in the blue sky, an airplane soars. The trees already have curling leaves, brown, red and gold fluttering in a light breeze. This is an ugly part of town, but there are beautiful trails by the river, where I've just decided I'll go. Maybe there I'll find some peace.

I pass the drugstore and realize I forgot to eat breakfast. My stomach tightens with hunger, so I duck inside to hunt for a chocolate bar, then take ages to select the one I want. I join the lineup to pay. The woman in front of me is chatting with the clerk about a store card. Just as well. I'm in no rush. I tune in and out of their conversation. Sometimes other people's conversations spark ideas for songs, but right now, the thought of writing a song makes me want to puke. I stare at a shiny nail polish bottle on a sale rack. I only have two dollars, and I don't seem to have my debit card. I tell myself I don't need it; I don't even wear nail polish with gold sparkles. But my heart is violently pounding from the stupid message. I picture Alec going under, imagine him watching me swim away, and now maybe never opening his eyes again. Because of me. And I need to do something to quiet my body. My brain. I glance at the store clerk, who's not watching me. There's no one behind me in the lineup. I can't believe I'm going to do this. I can't believe I *need* to do this. I can't stop myself.

My fingers pluck the bottle from the counter.

I close the nail polish bottle into my fist. Cold, hard, small. I push it into my jacket pocket, my heart hammering. A thrill charges through me, mixed with total stress. *What am I even doing? The clerk is going to know.* Now it's my turn to pay, so I slide the chocolate bar over the counter and say something like "Thanks" or "Bye" or "Have a good day." Or nothing. I can't even remember what I say, because I'm hurrying out of the store, stolen nail polish in my pocket.

I'm halfway down the block when the buzz comes. *I got away with it!* I check over my shoulder. *Yep. I got away with it.* Then all these other thoughts take over, like: *What the hell am I doing? Dad would be furious if he knew. This is dumb.* It's as if I can hear my brain arguing with itself.

I arrive at the river, where a solitary paddle boarder passes under the bridge. Traffic rumbles faintly as I lose track of time, watching the water, thinking of Alec going under, Suzanne crying out to me. I lean against a tree and take a couple breaths, my fingers playing with the little bottle in my pocket.

I press the fingertips of my other hand to my temple and sink to the ground, breathing in the smell of burning leaves from someone's backyard bonfire, and the words of the song from the day of the accident come back into my head. Suddenly the idea of working on a song doesn't make me feel sick; it makes me feel alive. I love the writer Anne Lamott. In one of her books, although I can't remember which one, she writes something about our worlds being small, something about the borders that contain those worlds. And how our worlds suddenly expand when we look at things differently. I let my mixed-up memory of her words seep into my mind.

I open up my cell. There are a bunch of messages from my dad and Lucy. They're worrying about me, about where I am. I should answer them, but instead I flip to Do Not Disturb. I let words whirl and grow in my mind, and I jot down possible lyrics: *We're caught off guard. It doesn't have to be this hard. Small, bordered worlds. Leave a taste but no trace.* After working on this idea awhile, I pull up the lyrics I wrote that day by the lake. There are some good lines in the opening:

Wanna give your heart to me
The fire in the woods
Cut down, cut down just one tree ...

A shattered moment
Take a sliver and look to see

Inside it's seven years' bad luck
The remnants of how we used to be ...

I realize that the first line, although I love it, doesn't fit in this song. Sometimes it takes a while to find the right opening, but I see it now. I cut the line and save it for a possible future song, and then I rework what I have left:

A moment in pieces
Take a shard of me
Look deeply inside for remnants
Of how we used to be.
Part the water, slide in a ripple
Find yourself in time
Find me.

A melody plays in my mind. The sound fills me up, pushing out Suzanne's desperate plea. I make more notes and then decide to turn to another song of mine — "Colony." Dad and I live on Colony Street. As I write, I imagine settlers bringing a wagon to the prairies, building a house with sod. Eventually I save everything, psyched about how much work I just got done. I can't wait to share this with the band; I can't wait to sing these songs.

My dad is digging in the front yard. He loves yardwork and gets sentimental about flowers. It's hard getting roses to behave in this part of the world, he tells me, and this fall afternoon, he tenderly prunes the rosebushes. The day has drifted away like the clouds overhead, leaving soft light. The heads of the flowers are droopy, and the air smells of their fading petals. He raises his chin at me.

"Not checking texts?"

"Sorry."

"Lark, I was worried about you. I came to pick you up after school — remember? We made a plan. You weren't there. Lucy told me you walked out before period three. She said you were a *total space cadet* before that. Her phrasing."

"I didn't remember you were coming to get me."

"What's going on?"

"I had to think." I switch my cell from Do Not Disturb and read over his messages so I don't have to look at him. "Yep, messages from you," I mumble. "And Lucy. And all the band. Sorry. Again."

"I bought sausages."

"Did you get any onions?"

"Everything on the list is there." He ducks back to his roses. I'm the cook in our house now, though after Mom died, neighbors and Reid's mom fed us. I sit on the front step, stretch my arms up, reach for the sky. My shirt rises, and the air tickles my tummy.

"I rewrote a song today, fixed a couple of lines. Worked on a new idea for another song, too, for practice later."

"That's really good." He plucks a stem of sage and passes it to me.

Holding the sage and inhaling its deep, warm smell reminds me of holding Alec's orange roses. I realize I don't know what happened to them. I lean back against the step.

"It seems wrong that Alec is lying *there,* and I'm sitting in the yard just the same as before our date."

"Lark, what you've been through …" he says gently. "Also … three years is hardly any time at all."

"This isn't about her."

"Of course it is. It was your *birthday*." He bends down and tugs out a weed.

We're both quiet. I get up from the step and feel my stomach grumble. For the first time since what happened to Alec, I'm *starving*.

"I'm going to make supper."

He grunts. "Next time we have a plan, put it in your calendar."

I laugh. "I don't have a calendar. You know that."

Although I'm groggy, I make it to practice at Iona's, and later, when I get home, I'm too awake to sleep. I wander to the bathroom.

As I stare in the mirror, memories of the lake intrude, and I make myself look into my own eyes, forcing the moment Alec went under from my mind. Next thing I know, I'm retching into the toilet, remembering how Mom once held back my hair when I was vomiting. I'm sweaty and crying and a total mess. I try to wipe up the splatter with toilet paper and then fumble in the cupboard under the sink to find cleaning product. My hand touches a box, which I pull out: it's hair dye, old stuff of Mom's — she used to love to change her hair. The color of this one is Smokin' Hot. Next to it is a box of hair bleach and a large pair of scissors.

I pull everything out and quickly clean up the mess in the bathroom. My stomach has settled, and suddenly my mind is clear of horrible images. I take a deep breath, but it isn't until I see the scissors in my hand that I realize what I'm going to do.

Alice Kuipers

Day 7: Sunday afternoon

I'm sitting on my favorite couch in Iona's garage, playing with the jewel on my belly chain, which dangles out over my jeans.

"You know what? I wasn't sure this week at school, but I like it," Iona says.

I touch my hair self-consciously. "Yeah. It seemed like a good idea at the time." It grazes my jawline and flops in my line of vision in a shaggy, Smokin' Hot red.

Nifty paces up and down. He puts his e-cig back into his pocket and presses the top of his nose.

"What's up, big man?" I ask.

He sticks his tongue out like he's dying of thirst. Then he shakes his head, which turns into him shaking his whole body. He works it out of his skinny arms and legs. "Let's get on with it. I just wanna play, you know?" He picks up his guitar and noodles.

Normally he plays bass guitar and I'm lead, but now he's playing the melody I sent him yesterday. He plays it first in F major, then again in D minor. The change gives it a different feel, exotic, sad, lost. The music fills the room, transporting me to strange lands, to a melancholia that only minor chords can bring.

"Play that again," I say, and I get up and do a couple of vocal warm-ups.

He waits until I'm done before he plays. This time I sing the opening lyrics of one of the songs I worked on by the river:

"I'm shattered glass
Shatter me, me, me

A moment in pieces
Take a shard of me
Look deeply inside for remnants
Of how we used to be
Part the water, slide in a ripple.
Find yourself in time
Find me
Part the water, slide in a ripple
Find yourself in time."

Iona slides in on the drums, a slow four-four. Then Reid comes in on keys, the notes ballerinas. He's an unbelievable player, so light and fluid:

"A tiny sliver enters
Turns my heart to ice
Shows me the way our life could be
Could be
Part the water, slide in a ripple
Find yourself in time
Find me ...

"Something, something, something ... I need a couple more verses ..." I sing, smiling over at the others. They keep playing. I finish up:

"Part the water, slide in a ripple
Find yourself in time
Find me."

Nifty adds a few bars of a possible harmony, lifting and joyful. The harmony is rough, but it *works*. His smile is infectious.

"Cool," says Iona, and she does a rousing drum solo.

The beat thrums through me.

Reid calls to Iona, "Sounds awesome." And then to me, "You too, Larkette."

It's been his nickname for me for years now, something to do with a nursery rhyme called "Alouette," which is about a lark.

I pick up the guitar I use for practice, Iona's old one, and play the notes that Nifty just played. We try them in the minor chord that was working so well, and I sing, my voice raspy in a good way. I fill the song with emotion and let my fingers lead the music, which swells and surrounds us. I'm nothing but the music. We build a little structure, and Reid adds another layer to the melody. He plays quickly, contrasting with Iona's slow beat.

We rehearse several of our old songs, and then I play my ideas for "Colony" to them. We try that out for a while, and then Iona takes off on the drums, so we just listen to the crash of her rhythm. When she's done, I bring up the show with Nifty. He's got something possibly for us in October. I insist we start to tweak the set list and fix our lineup. We've done a couple shows before, but this would be bigger for us — in a bigger venue.

Nifty says, "You're keen."

"We should make a huge deal of this — get out there more. We're really *good*, guys."

We take a break, because we're all sweaty and thirsty. Out of the blue, Reid says, "Saturday Drowning."

He has a habit of doing this, speaking as if there have been more words before, as if he's in the middle of a conversation that the rest of us aren't having. He glances at me and continues.

"It's been on my mind. I dunno. Maybe that's totally creepy. I know Sandcross is in a coma. Maybe it's creepy. Sorry ..."

He goes quiet. Only someone who knows Reid well would notice the faint flush at his collarbones. He pushes his glasses up.

"Yeah. Anyway. We could be something else, Larkette."

Alec not surfacing, the reflection in the water of the sky above, pain in my chest, Suzanne crying out, the water cold silk ...

I say, "It happened on a Sunday."

"Yeah, but Saturday sounds better," Reid replies.

I say, "It's a good name."

A sense of déjà vu comes over me, and nausea threatens. Everyone looks at me, eyes full of sympathy. I slow my breath.

"Guys, can we, like, sing or something?"

I start back on "Colony." My voice is husky and low. Nifty picks up when I break, and the others join in. A new verse comes as I sing, and when I get to the end, the rest of them cheer.

As I longboard down the street from rehearsal, Nifty catches up with me on his bike.

"You got a moment, Lark?"

"'Course." I stop and lean the board against a fence, scraping my knuckle slightly.

"So, Cole's parents are not cool with us."

"Seriously?"

Nifty stays on his bike, one foot on the ground like he might be set to zoom away. "Problem is ... Cole isn't ..."

"Uh, a few more hints might be helpful, Nifty. Cole isn't *what*?"

"Not answering. Cutting me off." He takes his e-cig and vapes.

"Those are gross," I say. I suck my scraped skin.

"I think he might be about to break up with me. His parents are BIGOTS." He stamps one foot. "And he should just stop being such a mama's boy."

"Why don't you say what you really mean, Nifty?" I reach up and squeeze his stick-man forearm. "But honestly, think about it. It might be hard for him. For them."

"Bullshit."

"Calm down. Your parents are cool, right? But they knew with you for, like, always." I let go of his arm. "You really like him, huh?"

Nifty nods, looking just like he did when he was four.

"Have you met his parents?"

"'Course."

"I mean, properly. Actually gone to their house — not just for a hookup with their son?"

"I like what you're saying here. A visit. Old-school social call?"

"Can't hurt. Or maybe even invite them to a café. Let them get to know you. Suggest it to Cole, and let him decide."

"Okay, I get it. Time for the Nay-man to man up."

"Okay, 'Nay-man.'" I roll my eyes and giggle. "Man up." I flip my board, which hits the ground with a clink. A distant car alarm goes off.

"Are you all right ...?" he asks. "You know, about Alec?"

I shrug. "I wonder if maybe we'd be together ... I mean, we were just getting to know each other. Nothing had happened. Yet." My face gets warm, surprising me, and then my eyes leak all over the place.

Nifty pulls me in for a hug.

"Shit, I'm sorry," I say, after I've cried against his soft jacket.

I draw away. "This is why the show's important to me. I want us to make the most of it." I gesture widely. "Of everything."

"Are you sure you're up to it?" He waves his e-cig.

"That still counts as addiction, you know," I say. "And yes, I'm surer of that than anything."

"These are cool, and you know it." He strikes a pose as if he's on the cover of *Vogue*, hip out, e-cig held in the air.

I laugh. "If you say so."

"You only wish you could be as cool as this." He points at himself. Then he points at my hair. "Though, now that you're rocking the nutty hair, you're getting there."

I shove him lightly, making his bike wobble. "Call Cole later. Tell him how you feel, but don't push. Suggest your plan. You might as well."

I put in my earbuds and push off on my board, bumping along the sidewalk as I listen to *Fox Confessor Brings the Flood*. It's old, and I love it — my mom loved Neko Case. As "Hold On, Hold On" starts, I find myself singing along, but then through my earbuds, I hear my cell. I come to a stop and flip up my board:

I want him to kiss me more,
kiss me harder.
I become liquid.

More words appear:

Nothing like Alec.
Nothing like this.

The message vanishes, leaving me cold in the dying day.

Day 13: late afternoon

Lucy passes me a J-cloth. Her hair is in thin braids, as if she's just come back from a beach holiday. "Thank the Great Spirit you're on with me tonight and I'm not working this on my own," she says. "I have a feeling we're going to be busy."

I plug my phone into the system. "Lana Del Rey, okay? I know — it's not cool to love her as much as I do." Her trippy, poppy rhythms bloom in the empty café. Music adds emotion to places, fills spaces, colors everything, and this album makes me smile.

Lucy weighs me up. "You're not on planet Earth tonight."

"I was working with a song, playing with it, sitting with the words, hearing the band riff on it, making it fuller. I haven't quite got the melody right, but I'll get there. It's on my mind all the time." I hum a few notes to her over Lana.

"I like it."

"It started the day Alec took me to the lake."

"You're going to do it as part of the set?"

"The show isn't a sure thing yet." I start wiping the counter in front of her.

She moves a dirty cup for me. "Nifty told me it was ninety percent. And I know you can make that last ten percent happen."

"I'm definitely going to make it happen." I hug myself. "A show will be so cool."

"Maybe one for your guitar?"

"Don't start that again."

"You love your Tak."

"Give me a break, Luce. Seriously."

She holds up her hands in surrender.

The door opens, and eight people come in, chatting loudly. "I knew it," she says, as even more people come in behind them, the lineup quickly doubling.

I look up about an hour later to see Martin Fields sitting by the window, staring out, his cell lying in front of him.

He catches my eye and says, "Hey! Hi, Lark! Wow. Cool hair."

I touch my bob lightly. "I'm getting used to it."

"I know Suzanne's been in touch, but I want to say thank-you, too."

Suzanne sent me flowers the day after the accident. And a card made by Annabelle. The flowers are in my bedroom, all of those petals drying. Martin jumps up and reaches out to shake my hand. He's stubbly faced — one of those cool, hip dads with his hoodie and jeans.

"I only did what anyone would."

"Yeah, but *you* were the one who did it. You know, Suzanne told me that Annabelle wanted to come and find you — she was the one who asked to go through the reeds. Then their canoe tipped." He shakes his head. "Alec ... right? I'm sorry he's still — have you seen him?"

"I've called a few times. There's no change. His parents don't want visitors yet. Only family." I shrug, trying to disguise that I'm hurt and frustrated.

Annabelle zooms in wearing pajamas, and Suzanne follows, curly hair in a bandanna; she's wearing a striped sweaterdress and knee-high boots. She kisses Martin and then notices me.

"Lark — it's good to see you. How have you been?" Her voice is gentle.

"Hi, Lark!" Annabelle clambers into a chair. "Dessert, dessert, dessert."

"Special dessert night," Martin says. "It's been busy with work."

"Talking about work — give Lark your card," Suzanne says to Martin. And then to me, "You're still writing songs? You should call and set something up. I kept meaning to mention it when you were our sitter."

I blush. Totally not cool. But Martin hands over a white business card with green lettering: MARTIN FIELDS, his number and email address. Nothing else.

"Least I can do," he says. "Really, anytime."

I take their order for chocolate cupcakes, milk and two herbals teas. Words for another song come into my head, words about what was nearly lost, about how different today could be for them.

Another customer walks up to the till. The Fieldses eat their cake and then leave into the deepening night, Annabelle turning back to wave at me. Then Lucy's mom — Dolphin — shows up. She's wearing a long blue dress patterned with small white flowers, with matching nail polish — even down to the tiny flowers. She comes over to hug me tight.

"Oh, Lark, honey." She sighs. Her voice is breathy. "Every single time I see you, I feel us going right back in time." She pulls away and inspects me. "Your hair. You cut it. Love the color. Your mom would have loved it."

I nod, wishing she'd stop doing this.

"You still look just like her," she says.

Dolphin and my mom were best friends for years. Now Dolphin can't seem to see me without seeing my mom.

Dolphin puts a hand on my cheek. "Oh, I feel her in you. You're a channel for her spirit."

I smile tightly. Finally, finally, she goes to chat with Lucy. She only stays a couple of minutes.

Later, after the last customer leaves, Lucy ties her bandanna over her hair and starts wiping up the kitchen, while I flip the sign on the door. The headscarf is multicolored and covered in jangly beads. It matches her long hippie skirt.

"I don't know what happened tonight. Bi-ii-iii-zzzzy." She wipes down the coffeemaker.

"Done now."

Lucy pulls a crocheted shawl around her shoulders. "Ready for Nitrogen Vice?"

"New Age-y, you say?"

"You'll love them. The main singer's got, um — what do you always say? Great lyrics." She catches the look on my face and giggles. "Trust me!"

"Where are they playing again?"

"Lydia's. I told you all this, Lark." She leans against the refrigerator, where she's just put the breakfast muffins she made for the morning. "You told me you're going to start living, right, until Alec wakes up?"

I chuck a cloth at her. "I don't know if Nitrogen Vice is living exactly."

"Uh, *seize the day* — that's what you said. Come on, they will have started already."

I pull out my cell, which has a new message:

Dad:
Wanna ride home?

Lark:
Going out with Lucy — okay?
Don't wait up.

Dad:

See you tomorrow night

— I'm out in the a.m.

Stay safe.

Lark:

Night. LU.

Lucy checks herself in the mirror hanging by the front door. The song I've been working on drifts into my head, and I make notes in my phone while Lucy finishes getting ready. She redoes her cherry lipstick and then turns to *Candy Crush*. I let her play, even though the Muzak from it is annoying as I'm trying to get the lyrics down. When I'm done, I pick up my longboard, and we lock up.

The moon is a bowl of milk above the chilly evening. Lucy lights one of her clove cigarettes, inhales and then exhales with a sigh of pleasure.

"That was the girl's family I was talking to earlier," I say. "You know, the day I went with Alec to the lake." My breath ghosts in front of me.

She grabs my hand. "The one you saved?"

"I guess so. I wonder what it would be like if I hadn't gone to her. Do you ever wonder about that?"

"About what?"

"I don't know. It doesn't matter. I guess there's no point wondering."

Ten minutes later, we arrive at Lydia's, where we flash our fake IDs. We're there so often the security guy doesn't even really check. Warmth and music wrap round me, and even though right away I can tell this isn't going to be a band I love, I relax. Lucy gets us each a vodka cranberry, and we settle into a booth.

"I'm making some plans I wanted to run by you. When we finish school." She takes a sip of her drink. "I'm going to nanny for a year abroad, I think. Make some money. Hit the road."

"That's so cool! Where?"

"I'm not sure yet."

"How about France or Italy?"

"Maybe …"

Reid walks in with a group of his friends. He nods a hello and makes his way over. He shakes his head toward the band, letting me know that he thinks they're as terrible as I do. The lead singer has picked up a triangle and is jangling it while humming into the microphone. I press my lips together so I don't laugh. The drummer looks like he's in some sort of trance, but Lucy is tapping her hand on the table to the rhythm, or lack thereof. The singer has a nice voice, though, and she's got good presence — the sort of person you watch on the stage, even if she is now sighing her words.

Reid puts his hands on our table and leans over.

"Isn't she amazing?" Lucy says.

He nods noncommittally, but he catches my eye, and his gaze reads: *We are way better than these guys.* A feeling of certainty buzzes through me. Our band is going to crush it. If we take it seriously, we're going to go sky-high.

Reid shakes his head as the singer puts her mouth so close to the microphone she's almost eating it. "Anika, Boh and Hollie … rumors they might play here in the summer."

"I know. It's exciting."

"I like the new song, Larkette. The last couple of rehearsals were great."

Something in his smile looks just like his mom's. I have a memory of Reid's mom and mine sitting together, drinking sugary black tea, talking and whispering, while Reid and I built train tracks across the floor. As we got older, he and I fought over the Wii. We would *Just Dance* like crazy — he beat me every time. Both our cells ping, pulling me back to the present:

The moon casts shadows
on Alec's face.
I just wanted to see you.
Be near you ...
He traces a pattern on my palm.

"What's this?" I ask Reid.

"What?" Our fingers brush as he takes my cell phone from me. "There's nothing there."

I grab it back and check. He's right.

"What was it?" he asks.

"A creepy message with no sender."

Reid lifts his glasses and rubs under one eye. He always does that when he's thinking.

"Isn't it weird your phone went off at the same time?" I ask.

"You think I sent you a creepy message? Come on, Lark, give me a break." He holds up his cell. On it is a message from Nifty.

I shake my head. "I'm being stupid. Sorry."

The mood is suddenly weird, and the singer is totally not hitting her high notes.

Reid says, "I guess I'll see you at practice tomorrow," and he walks back over to his friends.

I lean back in my seat and close my eyes. The taste of my drink is ashy, and my chest is tight. Who would send me a message like that? Why is someone trying to torture me? I put both hands on the table to steady myself, but the room is spinning.

Day 16: afternoon

In my room, I work with GarageBand. Then I do some vocal warm-ups before I sing a few lines of "Colony":

> *"We started with a blank page*
> *On it we wrote our story*
> *A case of something empty*
> *Before we added you to me ..."*

I layer drums beneath. Time disappears, meaning nothing, and when I surface, I flop onto the bed. I lie there, the duvet soft against my cheek, and I think about the day I hung 'my Tak on the wall. It was my fourteenth birthday. Mom and I were supposed to be going to get our nails done together — there's a place downtown that Dolphin goes to: she's obsessed with having perfect nails, despite all her hippieness. I'd been desperate to go, and we were going to meet Dad for my birthday supper at a Chinese fusion restaurant after. Then we had tickets for Neko Case.

I've replayed how that day was supposed to go a million times. Instead, that morning, Mom tried get out of bed, but she was too woozy, too dizzy to stand. She spent the day in bed; by evening, she was in the ER. She never left the hospital.

Raging at that birthday, raging at the fact that I didn't get to go to Neko Case, I put the Tak away.

Mom lived for only twenty-one more days. Cancer, when it makes up its mind to take you, shows no mercy. She had a tumor the size of a seven-month-old fetus. Impossible to remove without killing her, so they sewed her back up, leaving the tumor to spit vile cancerous cells through her major organs.

She spent her time writing me letters, making me a video, putting her affairs in order. Even when she was so weak, when she could hardly sit, she wanted to make it easier for us. She was that sort of a person — a doer, someone who made life happen, even as she died. And through it all, while I held her, I nursed an anger I could hardly stomach.

My Tak used to be the source, the way I blended my music and lyrics together. I didn't always know what I was playing, but once something sounded good, I'd learn the sounds and try to get it going and then go from there. Now when I need to noodle on the frets, I use Iona's old guitar, trying different patterns.

Words for another new song come to me:

Perhaps you see it differently
You and me
It's just a case of who tells the story
Perhaps you see it differently ...

Okay, I don't have a chorus or a bridge, but the hook line — *Perhaps you see it differently* — has that feel to it, like the start of a song that works. This will be the fourth song for the show.

Nifty:
Wish me luck.
I'm going over for supper
with Cole's parents tonight.
He told them it was important to him.

Lark:

Be your awesome self.

And a bit respectful — even if they're BIGOTS

— and say thank-you for the food.

Nifty:

Yes, boss.

Another message appears:

... let go of Annabelle's hand ...

Alec touches my shoulder.

No number, again. The message vanishes.

As I stare at the phone screen, tiny cracks appear over it. I touch it, and my finger comes away wet. What is happening? A voice — distant but clear — makes my head turn.

"Lark, are you okay?"

There is a static flicker in the air — I sense something before I see the shimmery shapes of a *room*. It's as if I'm looking through a window, through which I see a hospital bed. A little girl lies in it. It's *Annabelle*. By her bed, a figure moves: *Alec*.

Chapter Three

Chapter Three

Day 21: 8:00 a.m.

Alec and I wander over to a building called Twain Hall, which backs from the university onto St. Mary's Hospital. I remember looking out at Twain Hall during Mom's cancer treatment. It's four stories high, and on the fourth story on the side closest to the river is a random wooden beam — maybe half a yard wide — that sticks out but goes nowhere. I point it out to Alec as we sit on the too-cool, damp grass. I hear a message come in on my cell, and I check it:

> Alec, who is in a coma,
> who cannot be smiling ...

Another vanishing message. The words chill me. Alec in a coma? But it's not true. He's here, right here with me. I swallow back my fear and chuck my cell into my backpack.

I lie back, telling myself it's just a glitch, it means nothing, it's no big deal. The sky is soft blue, scudded with clouds. The smell of fall carries on the brisk breeze. But my heart is hammering.

"Hey," he says, climbing over me and rubbing one hand over my arm. "You okay? You're shivering."

"I'm fine," I murmur. "I just … you remember what I told you happened at the hospital when we went to see Annabelle? How I thought I saw her cry a tear? And the other stuff."

He nods.

"Well, I'm just —" I wave my hand at my backpack "— well, since the accident, I've been getting these weird messages about … well, about you, about stuff that isn't real."

"Messages?"

"But they vanish as soon as I've read them."

"Has anyone else ever seen one?" His dark eyes catch mine. "I mean, have you considered that the messages themselves might not be real?" Then he backtracks. "Just, you know, after the stress of what happened at the lake, perhaps — they feel real. I mean, they're real to you, but maybe they're not?"

"Not real?"

"You've heard of PTSD — post-traumatic stress disorder? We talked about that in psych class. There are a lot of symptoms … hallucinations and stuff."

"I've heard of it, sure." I sigh and let the quiet grow. After a minute, I shake my head to show I don't want to talk about it anymore. I can't get rid of the disquieting sense I've forgotten something important.

He pulls me toward him, and I rest my head against his chest. God, he thinks I'm a lunatic. His voice rumbles through me.

"Lark, I'm just going to say it. I really like hanging out with you."

"Oh …" I slide into the moment and let the feeling flicker.

"But really."

I hold his words like a small flame in my heart and kiss him.

He rubs his nose against mine. "It'd be good if this was serious. Between us."

I nod, the flame flicking and growing to create heat all through me. My mind says, *I love you, I love you, I love you,* but I shut it up. The word *love* has been coming to me all week at school. I want to tell him how I feel, but Lucy thinks I'm crazy. I remember the teardrop in Annabelle's eye, the image of my bedroom. I mentally shake my head: maybe he's right about the PTSD.

Alec kisses me, his tongue slipping into my mouth, opening me up. Things get heavy fast, and we're both breathing quickly when I stop and say, "We can't. This is way too public."

He smiles cheekily, his hands sliding down my body. He lifts my shirt out of the way to kiss the skin of my stomach. He murmurs, "Why don't you come to my house? Now?"

"You want your parents to 'nearly' walk in on us. Again?"

"They're away all weekend. Believe me, I checked. Triple-checked. Let's go."

"And leave that unclimbed?" I point at the ledge. "What sort of an urban ninja are you?" I grab my backpack, jump up and run to the base of Twain Hall. He tries to catch me, but I dart side to side out of his reach, so he gives up, laughing.

I drop my bag on the grass and, after three tries, hitch myself onto the ledge of the first-floor window, the cold concrete beneath me, the sharp edge of the wall pressing against my hip. I fumble for a jutting brick. I have to go on my toes to reach up, then hook my right foot onto a ledge and strain my biceps to heave myself up. I heave and haul, but my muscles aren't strong enough. I press against the wall, breathing hard. I shake out first one arm and then the other. This attempt, I manage to pull myself up. First one floor. Then another. The next floor is even harder — my arms are shaking. I pause to catch my breath again. Maybe I can't do this. Maybe I should just give up.

A flock of geese honk and flap overhead, heading south. Fall always comes early to this part of the world, but the geese seem to be leaving even earlier than usual; it's going to be a bitter winter. I watch them, anything rather than look down. Sweat beads along my hairline. Three floors feel a lot higher than they sound. Perhaps there is a slightly easier climbing spot at the other side of the window. I glance at Alec, one window along from me, and he nods in encouragement but doesn't speak. He seems to understand there's a need for silence. For focus.

As I shimmy along the narrow ledge, I glimpse my younger self standing in a hospital room across the grassy courtyard, watching Mom fall asleep with the bright-green chemo bag attached to her PICC line. I push away the memory and aim once more for the next floor up. I struggle to haul myself up to a projecting beam, fueled by the idea of my younger self watching me. Perhaps this is high enough for today — it's certainly high, and now that I'm here, the beam seems awfully narrow. I put a foot on it and walk a couple of steps. Then I carefully sit down to butt-shuffle along to the end.

Alec has swiftly climbed up behind me, and he frees both hands to clap when I finally balance myself, one leg on either side of the beam. I decide to show him a girl who isn't scared to do this — a girl I could be. Slowly, slowly, I stand. I hold my arms out. It's all a bit *Titanic,* but my heart soars.

"You're crazy." I hear approval in his voice and then his quick steps along the beam.

I giggle. "Crazy Lark. A whole new me."

He wraps his arms around me. He deadpans a line from the movie into my hair.

I giggle. "That old movie made me cry."

"I bet."

We can see the river from up here and a tapestry of golds, reds, maroons, greens and striking yellows. For a while we linger. Then it's my turn to follow him, as he scoots along the beam and down. It's way harder climbing down. I can't help glimpsing the too-far-away ground. My fingers hurt; my arms are trembling. My foot slips, and I slam against the wall, a groan escaping me.

"Jesus, Lark. You okay?" He's about six feet below me, terror in his eyes.

I pull in a shuddery breath. "I'm okay. I'm okay."

He climbs back up a little and helps me find better footholds, and I follow him down shakily. As I land, he yanks me to him and crushes me in a hug.

My cell sounds from my backpack, which I'd left on the grass, but I ignore it. It goes off again, so I unfold Alec's arms and get it:

Nifty:
Show secured!
Everyone in for brunch practice. You?
We need it.

Alec leans over my shoulder and says, "Is there still time to come to my house — you know?"

"Do I know?" I tease.

"Yeah. You know."

"Can I come by after practice? I should go. I skipped last Sunday because of you and Wednesday after what happened at the hospital, remember?" I turn to him and kiss him, lacing my fingers at the back of his neck. "I'll make it up to you," I say.

"Really," he says. "It's no big deal. You're worth waiting for."

"And you —" I giggle "— are getting the feels."

"You love it." There's that word again. He kisses me.

Eventually, reluctantly, I pull away. He leans over and whispers, "Maybe you could walk me home then go practice."

"I shouldn't."

"No, you probably shouldn't."

"Maybe I can be just a teeny bit late," I say, unable to stop smiling, as we walk. "I'll text the others soon." I chitchat about things I spot along our walk. A dog straining at its leash. A police boat on the river, which snakes below us as we turn onto Alec's street.

We arrive at his house. I've been here before, of course, but as the sun disappears behind a cloud, I notice how imposing Alec's house is, with two columns and a flight of steps to the white door. It seems old-fashioned, but it's actually brand-new, with a triple garage on the left.

Nifty:

Answer me.

Answer me.

"I gotta go," I groan.

Lark:
On my way.

Alec pretends someone is strangling him and falls dramatically to his knees. "No, no, no-o-o-o-o-o ... So close!"

"And yet so far," I tease. "I'll be back soon."

I lean over to kiss him while he's on his knees. He reaches up to hold my face gently in his hands. Then he pulls me to him, harder. He tangles his hands in my hair, tugging me, and because of the awkward angle, I stumble, bumping against the door frame.

"Ow," I say, laughing.

Alec gets up from his knees.

Nifty:
Sweet. See you in ten.

I slip my phone into my pocket. I still have a couple of minutes. Alec pulls me fully into the house and pushes me against the wall. I melt into him. I am honey stirred into boiling water.

"I've got to go rehearse. I can't miss it again," I murmur. "Next time."

"I'm not stopping you. Go. Go. Go." He lifts my shirt and begins to undo my bra.

I wriggle free.

He puts both hands to his throat again and feigns dying.

"I'll be back," I say, trying not to laugh. "I'll be as quick as I can."

*

Nifty and Iona won't let it drop — moaning that I'm hard to get ahold of, that I show up late, that I haven't been focusing, that I haven't been writing any new material, that even my singing voice isn't as strong.

"Come on, that's not true," I reply, my cheeks flaming with fury. But I haven't been singing much, and the muscles of my throat are maybe a little underused.

Reid is in my spot on the blue couch, eyes fixed on his phone as he blatantly listens.

"Reid?" I go to stand in front of him. "Do you agree with these guys?"

He puffs his cheeks and expels a sigh. "Are you surprised, Larkette?"

I cross my arms. "Surprised that you're all giving me a hard time? Yes. I'm surprised." I stalk away from him to the corner by the door. The three of them stare at me like I'm an okapi at the zoo. "When you were all loved up with Cole, Nifty, we left you to it."

"Ouch." Iona hits the cymbal. She rubs under one eye, smudging one of the three red stars she has painted there.

"Yeah, and look how that worked out." Nifty toys with his e-cig, gaze down.

"What?"

"We broke up, Lark. Like, yesterday."

"Why didn't you tell me?" I remember a couple of weeks ago he had asked for my advice about something, but I forgot about it.

He keeps his gaze down.

"I'm really sorry, Nifty. But — and I'm not trying to be a

bitch here — we gave you space at first, right?" I lean against the wall. "And what about you, Iona, when you're busy with Roller Derby? Or you, Reid, when everything was all about that coding competition? Or when you were puppy-eyed over Sharbat?" Reid glares at me. Something clicks. "Is that why you don't like Alec, Reid? You're jealous that he dated Sharbat and you didn't?"

"Sharbat switched schools after breaking up with Alec."

"Her parents made her. They didn't like him."

Iona comes around the drums and puts her arm over my shoulder. "Ease off. Enough rumor mill, Reid. And Lark, listen, Reid doesn't have a problem with Alec. We're just saying you've missed practice a lot — you missed it on Wednesday and blew it off last week. We've got a show in three and a half weeks."

I shrug off her arm. "I like Alec. Like, really like him."

Iona laughs. "Uh, wanna articulate that, songwriter? Like, do you like him? Or really like him? Like."

"This isn't funny."

She squares off. "I'm not joking. Songwriters write about what's happening to them — think of the great love songs. But even a terrible love song would be better than nothing."

Nifty puts his e-cig away and waves his guitar between me and Iona. "I know what it's like, Lark. At least, I did." He presses his hands to his heart and pouts dramatically. "But," he cries, "my darling, gorgeous songwriter, we need you now. The show is coming up. We've got no new songs. Not even a name."

"'Saturday Drowning,'" Reid says.

We all look at him. I swallow hard.

"I mean ..." Reid flips his phone over in his hands. "I've been thinking about that little girl. Trying to honor her. I want the band to mean something, to say something."

"It's good." I use the wall for support as my eyes fill with tears. "Shit, guys, I'm sorry. Something's wrong with me today." My phone announces another message; again there's no sender:

The shift — we're suddenly, truly, a band.
I hug Iona hard.

A spider walks up my spine, each tiny leg a shiver. At exactly that moment, I catch a glimpse of the date on my phone. No. Today. It's today.

"What? Alec just messaged?" Iona whines. "You gotta go?"

"Nothing like that." Anger scalds me. "Fair enough — I've been a crappy bandmate. But I'd forgotten … just leave it. I've gotta go."

"Lark, come on, I didn't mean …"

I hurry out of the garage without even looking at them. I can't believe I forgot what day it is. Anger at myself and memories of Mom fill my mind: I'm watching her onstage, the crowd hot around me. I'm fighting with her about a sleepover at Lucy's. She's bursting through the water at the pool, shaking water from her hair, smiling at me. I run as fast as I can, cursing that I don't have my board, and slam through the front door of my house.

Dad appears from the kitchen, rolling up his sleeves. He takes one look at me and grabs me in a hug. "It's okay, honey. It's okay."

Dad and I walk to the cemetery like we do every year on the anniversary of my mom's death. He asks, "Any news of the little girl? Annabelle?"

"Suzanne replied to a text yesterday. There's no change. I'll call again later today or tomorrow and see if I can go and visit." I haven't told Dad how weird it was last time. I'm not even sure I want to go again, so for the moment, I'm just letting the idea of a visit slide.

He winces, and I turn to him. "What's wrong?"

He brushes off my concern with a wave of his hand. "I'm fine. Just a little …"

"A little what? Is it your heart?"

"Maybe a tiny flutter. It's fine, Lark."

"We should go to the doctor."

We reach the cemetery. The fall is turning everything now — some of the trees have lost all their leaves, and the ground is littered with their bodies; spindly branches reach like a river delta to the crisp sky, and the grass is turning brown.

"Honey," Dad says, "don't worry. I'm fine."

"Tell me if it happens again. Okay?"

He nods. Our feet lead us to the place where my mother's ashes are scattered. She wanted them to be in a quiet corner under an elm tree, next to a row of wild rosebushes, the leaves of which are now furling in. Dad told me he had thought she'd want to be flung from a boat in the ocean somewhere exotic, or from the top of a mountain, something free-spirited, but she said that more than that, she wanted to be near us. Near me.

I hug myself. "I wonder what it would be like if she hadn't died."

He puts his arm around me. A breeze flips up leaves, and they swirl around us. "Your seventeenth birthday letter. I have it here." With his free hand, he pulls an envelope from his jacket pocket.

"I wondered if there was one." I've had two other letters from her since she died — one for each birthday. And one video, too. Her death came so quickly in the end, Dad told me, that she didn't have time to make more.

"After what happened on your birthday, and with you being busy with Alec, I decided today would be a better day to give it to you." He hands me the envelope.

Lark, My Daughter.

Dad squats by the grave and picks up a stick, which he traces through the grass.

I hold the letter to my nose automatically, but there's no smell other than paper and that gummy stuff to seal envelopes with. I imagine Mom licking this envelope, sealing it shut. I open it and read:

Dearest Lark,

I look at you now, fourteen years old, your face full of worry, which you try to hide from me, your body throbbing with anger. When you open this, you'll be seventeen years old, and I'll be gone. I can't imagine now not being there for you, and I'm so sorry I couldn't be there to mother you, to hold you, to help you grow into the woman I know you're going to become. I would give anything right now to stay.

But I can't. All I have to leave you with is my love.

My eyes blur with tears.

Listen to the quiet of your heart. Follow it. The world is more layered than it seems, and in those hidden depths, you'll find yourself —

Dad coughs. "Uh, Lark ..." He sighs. Then he clears his throat again. "I ... uh ..."

I shove the letter into the pocket of my jeans. "What's happening?"

"I feel a little — the flutter is back."

"We need to go to the hospital."

He nods. That's when I get scared. Dad never wants to go to the doctor.

"We don't have the car," I say, stating the obvious. He doesn't reply but sits on the bench and sighs again. He closes his eyes.

"Hey, it's going to be okay. Should I call 911?" As I say it, Dad puts his hand to his chest. I wish Alec were here to help me. "Dad? What do you want me to do?"

"I'll be okay in a moment."

I try to call Alec, but he doesn't pick up. After staring blankly at my cell for a couple of seconds, I call Reid. He answers right away. "Dad's feeling pretty bad. I'm not sure what to do."

"Where are you?"

"At the cemetery."

"I was going to head over there in a bit — I like to pay my respects. But I'll drive over right away."

I sit in the small waiting room of St. Mary's Hospital, on one of the three worn-down leather sofas. A TV babbles in the corner.

Reid is next to me on the sofa. After Dad was taken through

to be looked at by the emergency room doctor, Reid took hold of my hand. I hardly noticed at first, but now this detail focuses me. His hand is a lifeline.

Alec's voice breaks through to me. "Lark?" He fills the doorway.

I drop Reid's hand, burst into tears and rush into Alec's arms. His jacket is wet.

"It's raining out. Huge storm," he says. "How's it all going in here?"

"I think we're doing okay, but I'll be glad to have an update."

Alec kisses the top of my hair.

Reid stands and straightens his glasses. "It's been a long afternoon," he says.

"I was worried — you were supposed to be coming over, but you vanished," Alec says to me softly. "You didn't reply to any of my messages. In the end, Lucy got back to me."

"Sorry. I'm really sorry. I wanted you here so badly. I just … I meant to message you back … time just went …"

A doctor with white hair and two different-colored eyes — one milky blue, one deep brown — sticks his head round the entryway. He speaks quickly, like a rapid drumbeat.

"Lark Hardy? Your dad's a lucky man."

Lucky man lucky man lucky man.

"He's okay?"

"He's sleeping now. He had A-fib, which is normal for him — we'll need to adjust his meds. Anyway, it made him dizzy, but he's okay. You guys bringing him in saved the situation from getting worse. We had to …" He launches into medical speak.

"Can I see him?"

His drumbeat speech stops. "Of course. He's resting but

doing well. We're hoping to have him out of here tomorrow."

Alec takes my hands. "Do you want me to come with you?"

"Yes," I say.

"They said he's going to be okay. Remember that."

"I'll go and call everyone," Reid says. "Let them know what's happening."

I nod and follow the doctor.

The nurse guides us to a small room. Alec rests his hand at the base of my neck — it feels like he's holding me up.

The nurse smiles warmly. "Lark, are you doing okay?"

I don't answer. My dad looks as if he's just having an afternoon nap.

She says softly, "He's doing great," before she leaves.

I reach for Dad's hand, but gently, so as not to wake him. His skin is warm, and I squeeze his hand with relief while Alec rubs my back. A while later, Alec goes to get coffee. Sometime after that, another nurse comes in and suggests I go home and get some rest. I take one last look at Dad, who is still sleeping, and reluctantly agree.

Lark:
I'm heading back to
the waiting room.
Xxxx

Alec:
Okay.

I'm deciding whether to go right or left when I spot Suzanne coming out of the Pediatric Intensive Care Unit. Her eyes are heavy with dark circles, but she smiles.

"Visiting hours are over. You can come another time, Lark."

"No. I'm here … I'm here because my dad had a heart thing happen. He's fine. He's sleeping."

"Oh. I had no idea." She hugs me. "I'm sorry."

She smells of coconut body lotion. I remember that she always bulk-ordered the stuff.

"But I'm glad he's going to be okay."

"How's Annabelle?" I ask as we pull apart.

"The same. I wasn't really doing anything — just going for a walk. I've just got myself comfortable with leaving her room for short bursts. For a while, I was convinced she'd wake up if I left." She surprises me by saying, "You know, I'm sure I could slip you in now to see her, even though visiting hours are over." She gestures at the Pediatrics door. "It's so quiet at night — no one will notice."

"I'd like to see her." I remember how that tear appeared in her eye last time. "But I've … um …" I remember the vanished watermark. "Alec's waiting for me. I'll come and visit soon. I promise."

"Okay, sure," Suzanne agrees, her tone cooling slightly.

I walk away, bile in my mouth, disappointed with myself, toward the waiting room.

Lark:
You there?

Alec:
Here. Ur other friends came.

Lark:

Who?

Alec:

Band. Lucy.

Said they all love your dad ;-)

You okay?

Lark:

Be there 1 min.

Tell the others all okay.

Alec:

Told them already —

told them I'd stay with you

and they could go.

Okay? I'm here.

Lark:

Thanks. Yeah.

It's no big deal, I'm just tired

so glad not to have to visit with them all.

Happy you're here though.

When I get to the waiting room, I lean against Alec, still annoyed with myself that I don't have the guts to visit Annabelle.

He strokes my hair. Says soft things like *"You smell good"* and *"I'm here."* Then, "How's your dad?"

"He's fine. I'm a bit emotional — having Dad here, it reminds me of … when I was here, it was because of my mom," I say, letting out a deep sigh. "I'm just really glad you're here."

He kisses me, lightly at first, then deeper. Everything but the kiss disappears.

Day 24: lunchtime

Alec:
We need to talk.

Lark:
Like last time you needed to talk?
I don't remember much talking happening ;-)

Alec:
I'm serious.
But I don't know how to say it.

Dad calls from upstairs. "Lark? Are you coming?"

His voice is strong, and I smile, trying not to overanalyze Alec's message. This week everything's been fine with him, but I've been so busy looking after Dad that I haven't seen him much outside of school, and even there, I've been distracted.

"On my way," I call up.

"Don't bring me soup. I only want water."

"Too late." I put a slice of sourdough bread next to the chicken soup I tipped out of a can I found at the back of the cupboard and warmed up. I haven't done much cooking without Dad grocery shopping for me. Reid's mom has brought over a few things, though. And Alec brought the bread over yesterday. We had time for a quick kiss and a few minutes' conversation. His message probably doesn't mean anything — I'm reading too much into it because I'm tired and stressed.

My phone rings, and for a moment I don't look at it. I don't know if I want to hear what Alec has to say. There's a small grip at my heart, like a creature with tiny hands has seized hold of it. I pocket my phone, which goes off again, and carry the tray up to Dad's room. He's propped up in bed with his phone in his hand and a book discarded on his bedside table. I glance at the space next to him, where Mom used to sleep.

He says, "Tomorrow, I'm done with resting." Then he yawns.

"If you say so."

"They've gotta get these meds worked out so I'm not so tired."

"You love playing the wounded soldier, Dad."

Putting his phone down, he pats the bed. I place the tray on his lap and sit gingerly next to him.

"I'm serious. You've been amazing, Lark. But I'm okay."

"You might not be." My eyes settle on my grandmother's quilt, on a square patterned with clocks. She loved clocks — antique ones, brand-new ones, bird ones, all kinds. Her house was full of the *tick-tick-tock* of clocks on every available counter space and wall. When the hour arrived, every hour, a crescendo of cuckoos and bells would drive the rest of us crazy, but Grams thought it was marvelous.

"Something might happen, Lark," Dad says. "We have no control over life and death. Since your mother died, that's been …" He falls silent.

Dad and I both know that if we could have found a way to save Mom, we would have.

I sigh. "It's not just what happened to you. Actually, Alec just sent me this." I hold up my phone, the screen facing my dad. "It might be nothing, right?"

"Are you showing me your messages, Lark? Sweet." He frowns. "What does it mean?"

I turn the phone:

A tear slides down her cheek.

I really … hope he was happy.

"Song lyrics?" he asks. I shudder. This is the fifth message like this in the past three days.

But it's the only one that anyone else has ever seen. I was starting to think I was imagining them, like Alec said — hallucinating phone messages. A sob escapes my lips.

"Hey, Lark, what's going on?"

"I don't know. That wasn't even what I was trying to show you — oh, God, it's freaking me out. And on top of that, I feel bad because Suzanne asked me to go and see Annabelle, but I couldn't, because last time I got weirded out. And now Alec is saying we need to 'talk,' and I really like him, and you almost died."

"Whoa, whoa, my sweetheart. One thing at a time. I didn't almost die. I had a flutter. You know that. I'm perfectly fine." He smells of his shaving foam, and his pajamas are warm and soft as he hugs me.

"It was a scary flutter."

"All this fretting is bad for my recovery," he says softly, but teasing me. "You've only been dating Alec, what … a month? Even if it doesn't work out, you'll be fine." He holds my hand. "You're much stronger than you know. Like your mother. She looked like you could break her by sneezing, but she was the strongest woman I ever knew. Until you. You need to read her letter."

"Her letter? Oh, right. I forgot about it after the cemetery."

He chucks me on the chin. "Go get it."

"It's in the pocket of my jeans, I think."

In my room, I search through the pile of clothes until I find the jeans I was wearing. Then I pull out the letter and return to Dad's room.

"It's here," I say, and lie next to him. I pick up reading where I left off at the cemetery:

> Listen to the quiet of your heart. Follow it. The world is more layered than it seems, and in those hidden depths, you'll find yourself.

> *There is a dream I keep on having.*
> *One world made into two,*
> *but you only need to look in the moment.*

I look at Dad. "Are these song lyrics?"

"It's a song she was writing for you. She never finished it. She was very tired sometimes, writing these. I'm not sure it made much sense."

> *A life beyond*
> *Or behind*
> *Another way*
> *To find you*
> *If only that could be*
> *Only this course for me, only this life*

> *I am with you every step,*
> *even though you can't see me*
> *Believe me.*
> *I love you.*
> *Mom*

A coldness comes over me slowly, starting at my throat and passing through my body. What does her song mean? Her song lyrics have unpeeled something inside me, a truth, a fear, and I don't know what's going to happen now that I've read them. Everything looks different; everything is different. But, of course, it isn't; nothing has changed except for my mind roaring like a car engine before a race, a hum like an amp before the music starts. Before I can begin to get a handle on my thoughts, I hear my phone. Automatically I glance at it:

Alec:
You there?

Before I can write anything back, a message appears:

You're just jealous Alec
got to go on a date with me

Another message. A million tiny goose bumps. I want to puke. This creepy sender is scaring me.

Dad says, "Lark?"

Alec:
Come meet me after school tonight …

I message Nifty:

Lark:
I know we have the show, but I'm just not up for practice tonight.
Sorry a thousand times.

Nifty:

Send your dad a hug.

I message Alec:

Lark:

See you at 5.

I say to Dad, "Is there any more to the song?"

"That's all she had for your seventeenth. Why, you want to finish it? Make it work?"

"Something like that. Hey, you okay with me going out later?"

"I'm more than okay. But worried about you. That's what teenagers are for, right? Being worried over."

"I'm fine. And I'll go back to school tomorrow. And don't worry. I won't be long with Alec."

"I assumed you'd be going to band."

"Maybe on Sunday. Not tonight."

Evening is falling softly, creeping up on us. Alec sits on the teeter-totter, the other end pointing up. His eyes shine with something that makes my stomach quicken.

"I want you to come here," he says, and I feel undressed, my shirt unbuttoned, my zipper undone.

I reach the teeter-totter, and he tugs me to him. His arms are strong, and he pulls me onto his lap, my legs astride him. Then he leans me back so I balance along the teeter-totter. It's the sort of maneuver that could easily end up with me falling, but I don't, even as he lies on top of me. He's breathing warmly into my neck, kissing me just at the base of my ear, and every pore is opening, ice trickling down my spine, as I help him tug at my jeans.

We both fall off the teeter-totter and land with a hard bump on the sand, and I start giggling. "Yeah, let's make out in the play park," I murmur.

"You can't say we didn't try."

"At least there aren't any kids around." I shake sand from my long hair as I sit. "So, what's up? I thought you actually wanted to talk this time. You had me worried …"

"I do. Then when you arrive, I get distracted —"

My phone interrupts.

A video this time. It's of me sitting in the play park. I turn to look over my shoulder. Someone is filming me here? No. It's almost the same, but everything's different. In the video, I am lying on the teeter-totter, reading my phone. I have short red hair. And I'm not with Alec. Reid stands there. He leans over me. Suddenly audio comes on. In the video, Reid says, "Uh, Lark, what's wrong … I mean … everything okay?"

I stand up. "Who's doing this?" I shout. A whisper of wind in the bushes meets my cry. I run over, but no one's there.

"What's going on?" Alec stands, looking confused.

"I don't know. Someone sent me a video … Reid was here with me." I walk back to him and hold up my phone.

Of course the video is gone.

He nods. "Ah, Reid," he says softly. "That's what I wanted us to talk about. I mean, that's why I asked you here."

"You wanted to talk about Reid?" I'm still reeling from the video. "Why? What?"

"I saw you holding his hand. At the hospital."

"Seriously?" The question comes out more sharply than I had intended. "Nothing's going on with me and Reid."

He sighs heavily. "Are you sure?"

"Are you jealous, Alec?" I try to tease.

He fixes his eyes on me. "I'm maybe a bit jealous. Not cool, I know." His gaze is serious. Tender.

The feeling I have for him rises in me. That same tenderness. I say, "You trust me, right?"

"I do." The air thickens between us.

"I can't think straight right now. I got this letter from my mother with strange lyrics in it. Then I started thinking about stuff, you know, stuff that's been going on with me. Then this video. I'm sorry if I'm acting ... weird."

"Is this weird like what happened when we went to see Annabelle that time?"

"Post-traumatic stress? Maybe. But Dad saw one of the messages. I'm not making them up. Though I know that sounds crazy." I pout and hope it's cute. "I'm sorry that you're seeing a crazy person."

"My kind of crazy," he says. "Look, don't worry. We're fine. I'm fine. And you're perfect. You're just worn out with everything that's been going on — the accident, your dad, the anniversary of your mom's death. Hey, I've gotta take my truck over to my uncle to get some work done, but maybe I could come see you before you go to sleep." He kisses me on the hand.

"Sure. That sounds good."

I listen to Wyvern Lingo on the way home. Their voices calm me, make everything seem less spun out.

When I get home, I find Lucy sitting next to my dad on the front porch in the quiet evening. The smoke of a nearby bonfire drifts over.

"You're not supposed to be out of bed," I say to my dad. "You," I say to Lucy, "should have sent him back upstairs." I haven't seen her for a few days, and I'd forgotten how nice it is to have her around.

Dad stands and stretches like a cat. "There's nothing wrong with me that a little fresh air won't fix. I actually feel much better than I did lying around in bed. Oh, and I ended up finding a couple of other pages with notes from the same song, I think."

"Thanks."

"I'm going to go for a walk. I've got a hankering for one of those sports drinks."

"You should have told me. I'd have picked one up for you."

"I did tell you."

I check my phone. There's a message from him there. "Sorry, I missed it."

He starts down the path.

"Dad, let me get it for you."

"Stop, Lark. Everything's fine."

Lucy passes me a bag of chocolate-covered raisins. "I bought you these."

Mom used to love these chocolate-covered raisins. I'd forgotten, but we used to take them to the hospital, and she'd put one in her mouth and let it dissolve on her tongue. Sometimes they made her throw up, but when she felt a bit better, she'd pop in another one.

"Thanks."

I think about Alec in the park. The horrible video. Who could have sent it? Why? How? Oh, God. I hope I wasn't too crazy for him. But he said everything was fine, that I was perfect. I'm glad he's coming by later.

"You can talk to me, you know?"

"Talk about what? Sorry, I was just thinking about Alec."

"I bet you were." There's an edge to Lucy's voice. "You know, Lark, I'm trying to find a higher meaning in all this, but if you won't even talk to me, I can't figure out what that higher meaning is."

"What higher meaning?"

"I know you're going through a lot." The words spill from her. "I understand about your dad. For sure. But I'm getting the sense — something weird is going on with you. You and Alec, okay, I get it, you're in lurve. But it's you. You're different. Is something wrong? I just want you to talk to me."

I stand and rub my head. "I don't really know what you mean by 'different.'"

She stands, too. "Neither do I. It's just this sensation I'm getting — a vibe."

Alec:
You okay? I can't make it tonight — sorry.
Gonna be here awhile with my truck.

Lark:
Never mind.
Xxx

I hold up my phone to show her. "Do you think Alec's

avoiding me or genuinely having to deal with his truck? I was a bit, er, full-on at the park."

She doesn't look at the screen. "Lark — we're in the middle of talking …"

"Talking?"

"About what's wrong with you."

"There's nothing wrong with me. I'm just dealing with stuff with my dad, with some stress since the accident at the lake." I watch her purse her lips, which means she's trying to keep herself calm. "This is not about you, Lucy."

"I'm not trying to make it about me."

"Yes, you are."

"Will you listen to yourself, Lark? I try to be the best friend to you that I can, but you don't make it easy."

"Just back off, Lucy."

Her eyes widen in surprise.

Dad appears at the end of the path, drinking a sports drink. "You girls okay?"

"Fine," I say, thrumming with irritation.

Dad walks past us into the house. "Don't you have homework, kids? When I was young, I had so much homework."

"I've done it," Lucy replies. She picks up her bag and checks her phone. "But I do have to get to D'Lish. I'm going to be late."

I check mine, too.

Alec:

See you tomorrow, babe.

Hope my crazy girl's okay xxxx

"Homework. You're right, Dad."

I don't even bother saying goodbye to Lucy. I can't believe she's giving me a hard time, with everything else that's been going on.

I follow Dad inside, where I hurry up to my room. There I find the song notes from Mom that he's put on my bed. So, forgetting Lucy and her issues, I begin to read.

Day 27: Saturday, early

I wake early with my mind playing a melody to Mom's song lyrics. The past few days and nights, I've been replaying the words in my head. They've slithered into my dreams and made me distracted and forgetful at school, around Alec. And I've been Googling endless stuff about other people's phone glitches to see if anyone else in the world has ever had messages like the ones I've received — I had six earlier in the week, but no other videos, and nothing in the last two days.

I reach for the three handwritten, yellowed pages again. Her words are squashed in all over the place, and they don't follow the lines on the paper. Some of the words have been hard to make out among the doodles and arrows everywhere. It's how she wrote her lyrics; I remember watching her do it. But the song tugs at me — I feel like I'm not understanding something.

I flick through her pages. The last words I have are *I'm so sorry, baby.*

Before that, there's a cramped scribble that reads:

I'm struggling to get it in words
Struggling, too
To make it
To make it make sense
The words I'm looking for, in the dream
a second world, another life
I could have lived
Parallel you
Parallel me

Just the way it needs to be
You, me, if only ...

I groan and put aside the pages. I open up the notebook on my phone, start trying to write a song myself. The band have been pressuring me to come up with something. Sometimes songs appear swiftly; if I give myself five minutes, something happens. But this time, nothing comes. I can't just make a song appear out of thin air, and the air around my songwriting has been very, very thin. I check to see if Dolphin has replied. I feel bad about asking her for help now that things are weird with Lucy, but Dolphin might have insights on Mom's song — the song I can't get out of my head.

A voice behind me makes me jump.

"Lark?"

It's Alec, looming in the doorway of my room.

"Your dad let me in," he says. "What are you up to?"

I gesture to the pad of paper with scribbles on it — arrows and words to indicate sounds and song. "Trying to write. Meh. Nifty gave me a hard time again the other day. Said I needed to get them something new for Lydia's."

He sits on the bed, the mattress dipping underneath him. "Is it difficult? I mean, writing a song? How do you even start something like that?"

"You really want to know?" I ask.

"I do."

I pick up my pen while I talk. "The challenge is that you only have so much time and space. It's related to poetry in that way ..." I warm to my subject. "In a song, I'm trying to say the maximum with the fewest words. But at the same time, there

are differences between poetry writing and songwriting —
you're actually singing or playing."

"That makes sense."

I go to sit next to him. He smells of wood smoke and mint.

"The trick of trying to make a song come alive is reminding
myself it's not meant to be on the page."

"What does that mean?" Alec takes my wrist. Really slowly
he turns my palm up. He kisses the point where the doctor takes
a pulse.

My heart quickens. "I mean that, for example, a song like
"I Want to Hold Your Hand" is a brilliant pop song, but you
put those lyrics on the page, and the song looks — goofy. It's
not meant to be read. Songwriters have to understand there are
more dimensions to what they're doing — what the background
is going to be like, how the band's going to fill out the song,
what type of song it is. They also have to understand what a
good hook is and why it works."

"How do you know all this?"

"My mom." Her soft voice murmurs to me through time,
and for a moment I hear her sing. I say, "Not that I'm doing any
songwriting." I show him the blank page. "I haven't written a
single line of a song since the day at the lake. Even though I've
been trying — it's like I'm stuck. Writer's block. Urgh." I run my
hand over his hair. "Now, your turn. You seem a little ... quiet."

"I'm dealing with some stuff with my parents," he whispers
into my hair. "Lark, I want to tell you ..."

"But?"

He tips my face up to his and stares at me. His eyes lock on
mine.

My cell interrupts.

"It's okay. Deal with that."

"No, it doesn't matter. The stupid phone can wait," I say, though I hope it might be Dolphin.

"I don't really want to talk, anyway."

"I'm here when you're ready." I turn to my cell:

Tish:

Can you come in at 11?

"Tish just gave me a shift. I bailed on the last couple because of … stuff. But if you don't mind … I really could do with the money."

He reads the message over my shoulder. "Sure. We've got time before you start. Let's do something fun. You. Me. This room. How about it?"

"If I miss another shift, she might actually fire me."

"We've got loads of time. Trust me, baby."

… sleep is secretly stealing him
without him even realizing …

"I haven't had one of these for a couple of days," I say.

"Another weird message?"

"Just when I'm not expecting it. I don't even know what that one meant. Like, at all." Again I have the feeling that I'm missing something urgent.

"Let me help you take your mind off …"

I smile at him, inviting. Alec catches my look, and it ignites something in him — the spark between us, something. He pushes me down onto the bed. Before I can take a breath, he climbs on top of me, tongue and hands exploring my face, my body.

I want this — I want him; the impulse in my cells is to arch toward him, forgetting everything. And for a moment, my body does. But as I close my eyes, I see my phone with the messages on it; I see Annabelle's long hair spread out in the water.

"Hey, hey," I say, as he starts to kiss my neck. I wish I could just let go. I wish everything were different. "Easy, tiger," I say, pushing both hands against his chest.

"What are we waiting for?"

He groans. He grips my hands above my head, easily, with one of his hands. He has me locked down with his knees on either side of me, and he slowly unbuttons my shirt.

"Alec, stop."

"You mean it?" he whispers, licking under my ear.

Oh, it feels so good. But I squirm. "You know I want to, too, just not now …"

"All right, all right," he says, climbing off me.

"Just give me a little more time. Please? I'm just — It's the weird messages …"

"I guess I'm not distracting enough …" He flexes his muscles. "Though some women would go wild for this."

"I am wild for this." I giggle.

He stands up and moves toward the door. "You get ready for work. Then I can't be blamed for you not showing up."

"I've still got two hours!"

"I'm going to go train with the others. Work off my frustrations …" he says, and grins. "You drive *me* wild." He blows me a kiss at the doorway.

*

I give up on songwriting and message Nifty apologizing —
again — for not coming to band practice on Wednesday and
for not having a song for him yet. I wonder if maybe I should
just tell the band I don't want to be a part of the show this time.
Maybe the next one. But no, I should do the show, if only to get
me out of this weird headspace.

I grab a denim jacket and go outside, where the cool
gray air wakes me up. I've spent lots of time, especially after
school, walking alone by the river, feeling winter coming and
wondering if I am going crazy, debating over and over whether
the messages are really there at all … But then, how do I explain
the fact that Dad saw one of them?

Lark:
Ready, but too early for work now :-(

Alec:
Why don't you come train with me before you go?
By the river —
walkway under Victoria Bridge.

Lark:
Coming.

A text comes in:

Dolphin:
I'm away at a retreat this week.

How about next Thursday evening?

I check my schedule and text straight back:

Lark:
Of course.
I'll come by after work.
Around 9:30?
I haven't seen you for ages.

Dolphin:
You're right. It's been too long.
9:30 is perfect.

I hear Alec's friends talking before I come upon them: *"I would normally go this way when doing flips. Aim for the grass, then right back."* They come into view: Tyler, Logan and Jordan, standing around at the edge of the bridge along a walkway with several rails and a wall a little taller than Alec. In the light breeze, I hear Logan saying, *"I don't think I ever actually tried this before."* He runs, jumps, somersaults and lands on both feet on a narrow ledge.

As I approach them, a few drops of rain spatter me. A large truck roars by on the bridge. A couple of other guys, wearing baggy pants and colorful sneakers, farther down by the river, are saying, *"Don't land on the edge, man. That's scary stuff."* They're filming each other.

I look at Alec. He does his slow smile. For a moment, we're the only people there.

Then, like a lynx, he jumps onto a rail. "My main goal is to get a good grip in a cat leap," he says to Tyler.

"You're thinking too much," Tyler says.

Alec jumps down.

I kiss him hello. "Can I try something today?"

"Sure. Try the basic stuff to warm up, Lark, rolling, climbing. Then we can do some vaults."

I do all that, and he teaches me a wall climb. He links his fingers so I have a foothold, and I scuffle and scrabble against the wall, feeling pleased when I pull myself up on the third try. Alec practices something called "kong vaults" over a smaller wall. I manage a cool stunt where I bounce off a corner wall, my feet slamming into it. Then I try a few more wall climbs, until my hands are sore. When I jump down, Alec catches me before I hit the ground. He hugs me close and then pulls back.

"Good try, babe. And look —" he tips my chin so he's looking into my eyes "— if I was pushing too hard earlier —"

"You weren't."

"I've been kind of stressed but ... anyway, you take the time you need."

"It's not that I don't want to."

"I know. How could you not want to?"

He says it as a joke, but he looks vulnerable.

I kiss him, pulling him close to me, conveying with my mouth and body how I feel. "I should get to work."

"Come meet me later, after you're done?"

"I will. I promise." I put Saint Saviour on loud and walk away.

Suzanne:
Haven't heard from you for a while.
I hope you don't blame yourself.

Do you want to come
and visit this afternoon?

I groan as I read her text, pausing outside D'Lish. I could just ignore the message and not deal with this. But … I should go visit. I remember the vision I had last time — what if it was a panic attack? I've heard of those. What if that's what's been happening to me? I push the thought aside; I can't handle it for the moment. I message Alec:

Lark:
Want to come with me
to see Annabelle later?

Alec:
Dad just messaged.
He needs a hand with something.
You okay to go w/out me?

Lark:
'Course. I'll be fine.

Alec:
Miss you already, crazy girl.
X

I walk to the hospital after work. When I get to Annabelle's room, Suzanne opens the door with a puzzled expression.

"Is it okay for me to visit now?"

"Oh, I wasn't expecting you — you didn't reply to my message. But of course."

She twiddles the ends of her hair. It's a girlish gesture that she doesn't even seem to know she's doing.

Annabelle lies in the bed, eyes closed, the machine beeping to the rhythm of her heart. The room smells of dead flowers. The flowers in vases around the room are the same ones that were here last time. Suzanne follows my gaze.

"It's me. I won't let them take the flowers away. I can't —" Her voice cracks. "Sheesh, Lark, I'm going to stop crying every time I see you, promise."

I sit next to Annabelle. For a while, we sit there in silence. Nothing happens. See. I'm fine. Everything is fine. Then I'm hit with guilt. This isn't about me. This is about a very sick little girl and the fact that I didn't save her.

Suzanne stands. "Do you mind if I go to the washroom?"

"Sure." I shift in the chair.

"You'll be okay? I mean … after last time?"

"I'm okay. I'm fine."

"I'll just be a minute."

The room falls quiet again as the door closes behind Suzanne, and I match Annabelle's soft breathing. In and out. See, I'm not crazy. Everything is normal.

From a jug on the bedside table, I pour water into one of the foam cups stacked there. I sit for a few seconds, listening to her breathing. Then I reach for her little hand. Her skin is warm, alive. A shiver travels from her to me. But I hardly notice: all my attention is on the foam cup in my other hand. The water in it is darkening, becoming browner and rising. Water spills over the edge of the cup and is shockingly cold against my fingers. I drop the cup, and water spills over the cement floor, spreading rapidly. A few leaves and a long green strand of pond weed emerge from the fallen cup to drift into the deepening water.

I am stunned, paralyzed.

Then I feel a static shimmer in the air. Panic seizes me. I can't open my mouth to shout. In the air beside me I see, as if through a window, another girl.

We face each other. She has cool, jaw-length red hair. Just like in the video someone sent me. But everything else is the same. The face, the eyes.

It's — it's me.

Behind her, I see Reid ... and Martin Fields. They are in a white room.

Finally my voice returns, and I scream.

Chapter Four

Chapter Four

Day 21: brunch practice

Panic starts to wake me up at night. And wisps of lyrics. I call St. Mary's every couple of days. The nurses can't or won't tell me anything, but Alec's friends tell me there's no change. None of them have been allowed to visit either. Alec's parents just ask for space, for time. I keep thinking about what happened in my bedroom the other day. I lie in the darkness trying to figure out what it meant when I imagined seeing Alec standing in a hospital room.

During the days, although I'm tired from lack of sleep, I'm weirdly energized. Everything clicks at school, and I ace a history test with hardly any revision. Our Wednesday practice is good. I show up with two new songs for Sunday practice, which we start much earlier than usual. Normally we have practice at four, but because we're all so pumped, we decide on brunch practice at ten. Practice rocks, and as I sing, the bass notes from Nifty's guitar thrum through me. My fingers dance, and each sound touches me through my very skin. I close my eyes and let the words open me up, really feel the rhythm of Iona's drumming and Reid's harmony, as if we're all one entity. We're better than ever.

When we finish, we all know that something's happening. The shift — we're suddenly, truly a band. I hug Iona hard. We're both sweaty.

"I think we're going to make it," I say, pushing my short hair away from my eyes.

She nods. Nifty and Reid high-five each other.

It's one of those fall days when the sky is a perfect blue and there are only a couple of clouds, floating fluffy and white far above. I longboard along the river path instead of going home, and then I swerve toward Broadway. At the store, I walk past the fat, glistening vegetables, past the morning-made sushi. I'm still feeling high from practice. When my cell goes off again, I assume it's my dad, but —

You love it.
He leans forward to kiss me.
There's that word again.

The words are almost lyrics.

The message vanishes and is replaced by a short, looping video. It's Alec's *face*, close up, smiling, his dark eyes alight. I turn up the volume, but there's no audio. Alec, who is in a coma, who cannot be smiling in my cell.

I touch the screen, and the video disappears.

I linger over the empty screen, my lip quivering. What is

going on? I fight rising bile and shove the phone into my pocket and walk over to the pharmacy aisle, where I grab a tube of mascara. A quiet feeling of power rises up inside me. I tell myself I don't want mascara. Don't need it. But the pink packaging and smooth feel of it compel me. I don't let go.

Switching to a song by The xx on my cell, I keep my eyes down and move to the front of the store. I tell myself that I'll put it back, that I'm not going to steal, but the voice in my brain and my actions slam against each other. The mascara is in my pocket, and the doors to the store swing open automatically. I walk outside.

I flip my board and cross the parking lot, and the anxious feeling lifts, replaced by euphoria. I'm as sunny as the sky between the perfect clouds. I toss the mascara into a garbage can as I pass by.

When I get home, I'm humming a few bars of one of the songs I've been working on. With a couple of tiny changes, it would work better, I realize. The impulse to write and sing is strong, so I hurry straight upstairs. Something nags at me, a tickle inside my brain, but I can't think what I have forgotten. Instead lyrics drift in me about stories, choices, memories, so I begin a new song.

Eventually I surface. I pick up my cell and realize it's been on Silent. There are several texts from Dad. I'm just about to read them when another message arrives:

We reach the cemetery.
The fall is turning everything now —
some of the trees have lost all their leaves
and the ground is littered with their bodies

The words vanish, leaving me with a dry throat. The *cemetery*. It's the anniversary of my mom's death. And I *forgot*. No wonder Dad has been messaging me. I grab my backpack and am just about to race out the door, when my cell rings.

It's Reid. "Larkette?" He sounds strange. "I just found your dad at the cemetery. He's having trouble breathing."

I've been in the waiting room at St. Mary's Hospital for so long I've lost track of time. Lyrics slip through my mind, about life and death, about rooms where we wait.

"This heart thing — Dad told me it was under control. But nothing's under control, is it? Everything's random —" A sob catches in my throat.

Reid pushes my lipstick-red hair from my cheek.

"It's going to be fine. Your dad is strong."

He lifts his glasses off and rubs the skin under his eye with a knuckle.

"I loved your mom. Everyone did. She was so kind to my family when we moved here."

He presses his hands lightly around mine as if trying to give me strength.

"You probably don't even know all the things she did for us. She brought my parents bedding, introduced Mom to people, helped us find schools. Like a fairy godmother."

"Is that why you were at the cemetery?"

"I go every year. I mean, I make sure not to get in your way or your dad's."

I look at him for a moment. "You saved his life. What if you hadn't been there?"

A doctor with white hair and two different-colored eyes — one milky blue, one deep brown — sticks his head round the entryway. "Lark Hardy?"

"Oh, please tell me he's okay."

"Though we don't think he's had a heart attack, we're concerned about how hard he hit his head when he fell … It's fortunate your friend found him when he did." He launches into medical speak.

The refrain *heart attack heart attack* makes it impossible to hear.

I interrupt. "Can I see him?"

"You can visit for a short time."

I glance at Reid, who says, "Do you want me to come?"

I shake my head.

"I'll be here," he says.

I follow the doctor.

The ICU is a creepy vault of noise and silence. My ears attune to the sounds of breathing, the beeps of oxygen machines, the puff and fall of an artificial lung, the pad of feet, the gentle voice of a woman talking to someone who isn't able to reply. Those are the noises. But beneath is the silence of the people lying on those beds, hovering between life and death.

I see Dad — and almost wish I hadn't. They didn't tell me about the wires and tubes, the *machines.* I fix on the beat of his heart on a monitor even as my knees give out.

The ICU nurse, a slim woman with glasses, catches me around my waist and guides me to an armchair next to the bed. For the moment I sit, not looking at my father, not listening to the nurse, who is saying something to me.

When I do glance at him, my heart thuds. He looks *dead* — his face is ghastly pale, and his body as still as a branch on a windless day. I pat his hand. His skin is warm, and I find myself weeping with relief. I have been to a room just like this before, but I blocked it out. The memories come back now. My mother in a hospital bed. The images of the two of them blur together in my tears.

The nurse frowns. "Do you need a glass of water?"

"No, I'm okay."

When she turns her attention to another patient, I make up a couple of lines to sing softly to Dad. He always loves it when I sing:

"Just lying here
The way it's gone
You could be gone
I'd be alone ..."

I rest my forehead on his bed. Beneath the hospital smell is the smell of him, of my father.

A different nurse touches my shoulder and says, "Young lady, I hate to wake you, but you need to go now."

I don't know how long I've been asleep. I take one last look at Dad — his eyes are still closed — before I leave the ICU. I'm standing in the hallway alone, momentarily confused, not sure whether to go right or left, when I spot Reid. He walks up to me, hugs me, asks me about Dad, his voice vibrating through me.

"I'm glad I found you."

"Thanks," I say, as I pull away, "for everything. Do you think Dad will enjoy the show?"

His eyes try to hide his surprise, but almost as quickly, he seems to realize I need this. Now more than ever.

"The show? 'Course. He'll be much better by then. He'll love it."

Lucy rushes along the hallway. "Oh, Lark, how's your dad?" She hugs me, the smell of clove cigarettes curling from her damp hair.

"Why is your hair wet?"

"There's a wild storm, absolutely pouring rain. Is Nifty here yet? He messaged that he was coming. And Iona?"

"Nifty will be here in about ten minutes." Reid rests a hand on Lucy's shoulder. Her arm is around my waist. He says to me, "They all wanted to come as soon as we got here, but you seemed pretty out of it. Lucy decided everyone should wait until you had more news — she's been coordinating everything. You have a casserole from my mom in your fridge, and she's cleaned up your kitchen."

"How was the visit with Vince?" Lucy asks.

I might faint if not for her arm around me.

Iona:

I'm here. U ok?

Where r u all?

Why is no one answering me?

I remember Mom's funeral, and through the smudge of tears, through it all, Lucy, Reid, Nifty, Iona huddled around me. I message Iona back:

Lark:
Thanks for coming. Love u.

Iona:
Yeah, but where ARE u?
Am standing with man-freak
bleeding from face in ER.
Think he wants to eat me.

Lark:
We're going to wait room on 3rd floor.
See u there.

Together we walk along the hallway. Lucy holds my hand. A woman comes out of the door to our left. She's slim, glamorously dressed, with coiffed hair, but she looks tired. I realize it's Alec's mother. She stops when she sees us.

"Hello, Mrs. Sandcross. It's me, Lark."

"No visitors. Not yet."

"Oh, no. I'm not trying to … My, uh, dad is here." I point toward the ICU.

She barely nods. "Is he okay?"

"Maybe." I shrug. "But how's Alec?"

"Not good. They moved him from the ICU to his own room in Pediatrics, because he's not yet eighteen, about a week ago. For a moment, we were hopeful because they moved him. But the tests they've run don't look good. There are always stories, but as Scott says … we'll have to make a decision. His birthday is coming up — did you know that?" She worries her thumbs. Her gray wool dress has a small stain on the right hip.

Abruptly she turns, and her heels click along the floor away from us. I have a sudden insight that she's weeping as she walks. Another tiny piece of my heart crumbles.

I lean against Lucy. "I don't think I can handle any more."

Lucy murmurs into my hair, "Let's find Iona."

"Before she gets eaten alive," I reply, smiling wanly.

Day 24: lunchtime

I knock on Dad's hospital room door. He's sleeping with his cell in his hand and a discarded book on his bedside table. I take a Thermos from my bag. In it is chicken soup. I even made the stock from the chicken thighs I got Lucy to buy for me. Egg noodles float with the carrots and finely chopped onions, just the way Mom used to make it. I put the Thermos on the side table and carefully sit next to him.

He yawns as he wakes. "You should go to band practice today."

"I should be here."

"No. Lark. You should be prepping for the show. Then I have something to look forward to. You know, if I ever get out of this hospital room."

"At least you're out of Intensive Care now."

"I'm slowly going mad staring at these four walls."

"These four walls are a lovely shade of bile. Not that you were staring at them. You were sleeping — you need the rest, Dad, while they figure out what happened."

He pulls a face. "Okay, okay. But please go to band practice. And call Martin Fields. If we learn anything from this, it's to seize the day."

"Touché."

"Cliché, actually." He yawns again. His face grays a little, and he turns from me. He murmurs as he falls back into sleep, "Maybe I'll eat later. Now, get on out of here."

As I leave, I hear someone call my name. Alec Sandcross's mom is behind me.

"Lark —" she says. Her voice is soft. She's wearing a blue

cashmere sweater, a designer scarf, and her hair is pulled back in a braid. Her lips are perfectly glossed, mascara and liner emphasizing her very pale, almost silver eyes. "Do you have a moment?"

"Of course."

"I do hope your dad is feeling better. I'm sorry I was so … abrupt the other day."

When you were crying and didn't want me to see? "Don't worry. This place does that to people."

"It's just — could you tell me something?"

"Sure. What is it?"

She gazes at a spot I can't see for so long that I wonder if she's forgotten I'm there. Then she says, "What was Alec like?"

"We were only just starting to get to know each other, Mrs. Sandcross." A small frown travels over her tight brow, so I add, "He's smart. And interested in stuff. Always asking questions at school. I was happy he asked me to go to the lake. I was excited. We had lots to talk about. He seems dynamic, cool, um, I wish I knew him better. I'd still really like to visit him, you know. It felt like we would have … we could have a good thing. Maybe."

"Lark, I know … I know this is a strange question … but … was he happy?"

Though her voice is soft, her silvery eyes — intense under the makeup — still look tired.

"I hope … I hope he was happy."

The question floats between us. I don't even know how to answer — I hardly knew Alec. Wouldn't his own mom know if he was happy? Why would she even have to ask something like that?

"Sure. Yeah. He was happy. Of course," I reply, lamely.

Her gaze shifts to me. If anything, her focus becomes more intense. A small prickle begins at the top of my spine.

"I worry he has too much of his father in him, too much … I left him, you know. Alec's father. I should have done it a long time ago. It might never have happened if Alec hadn't been in here." A tear slides down her cheek. "I really … hope he was happy."

Suddenly her cheeks flush. She closes herself up like an app that is crashing.

"Goodness, listen to me. I'm … I'm terribly sorry to bother you."

I just want this to be over — and I hate myself for feeling this way. "He'll get better," I say. "He will."

"No, that's not what's going to happen. The tests are pretty conclusive. We're going to give things a little more time, but only until his birthday. Even if Scott and I can't agree on anything else, we agree that our son can't live like this."

My heart aches for her. For her family. For myself. "Alec's birthday?"

"Yes. Twenty-one more days … the doctors aren't hopeful." More tears threaten to fall.

I shiver. Twenty-one more days … that's the time I had left with my mom from my birthday to her death. "Can I come and see him with you?"

"Not today." Her gaze drifts away from me. "No, sorry. Not today."

In English class we discuss *Identical,* by Ellen Hopkins. It's a great book that I read over the summer, knowing we were going to study it, but I've got Jacob Parks — otherwise known as God's gift to the world — in my group. The lesson drags on. Iona, who's also in my group, is raging at Jacob by the end. She has a blue lightning flash painted across one cheek, and I imagine it sizzling. She's wearing a shiny lipstick that matches her red nails, with a tight black sweater, black pants, black over-the-knee boots. Her hair is a huge halo around her head, wild compared with her superchic outfit.

When the bell rings, I grab her arm and drag her out of there, but I can't stop her storming off to the principal to report Jacob's sexist input. She turns and blows a kiss at me with her very red mouth.

Lucy finds me and tells me about her new *Candy Crush* level, and then we chat about the after-school babysitting job she got to fit around her shifts at D'Lish. I tell her about the songs I've been working on.

Later, after math, Iona catches up to me as I leave the school.

"You calmed down?" I ask her.

"Don't even get me started again."

I pretend to cower.

She one-two punches the air. "See you at practice. We're rocking it."

Back at the house, I hunt for the jeans I was wearing when Martin Fields gave me his card at D'Lish. I'm terrible at laundry, so I eventually locate them in a crumpled heap under my bed. I toy with my phone but cop out. I spend a couple of hours writing notes for songs, and I do some vocal warm-ups until it's time to go to practice.

Reid arrives outside Iona's parents' garage just as I do. He asks about Dad. I tell him about today's visit to the hospital and about what happened with Mrs. Sandcross afterward, but I find it hard to articulate how sad it was. The great thing about Reid is that he gets it anyway.

"She must be messed up right now."

"I think so. She kept asking if Alec was happy."

"I hope you lied."

"What does that mean?" I walk into the heated garage with him. The Darcys are on superloud. Nifty is dancing around the far side of the room.

"The guy had stuff going on," Reid says over the music, leaning close so I can hear.

"What do you mean?"

Typically, Reid doesn't answer.

"You're just jealous Alec got to go on a date with me," I tease, trying to get him to reply. Except it comes out just as Nifty stops the music.

"So go on a date with me." His voice is loud in the silence.

Nifty cheers. And Iona, who I hadn't even noticed, bangs a drum. "He finally asked her!"

Did he *seriously* just ask me on a date? "Where?" I ask, torturing him a little but also feeling my heart buzz.

"Stop it," he says. Smiling. He adjusts his glasses. Again.

Both Iona and Nifty watch our conversation with way too much interest.

"Okay," Reid says, "time to get to work, folks. Don't we have a show to get ready for?"

Iona bangs the drum again. "Yes, we abso-fricking-lutely do."

✳

I try to talk to Reid when we finish our superb rehearsal, but he's on his phone. I wave, less sure now that he did seriously ask me on a date, and head out on my longboard to get back to Dad. I cut through the park. It's another clear day — as if winter is holding back, waiting to spiderweb frost all over the golden leaves and browning grasses — but dark is falling now. As I reach the play park, I hear my cell. I stop my board, check it and try to hold on to reality.

Because in a video on my cell, *Alec Sandcross* is sitting there. Right there in the play park. I rub my eyes, like, actually rub them, to make the mirage go away. Alec is in a coma. But there he is, sitting on the teeter-totter, one end pointing up to the evening sky. And in the film, on the other end of the teeter-totter, is *me. Another me.* But my hair is how it used to be, long and black.

I watch the two of them. On the screen, Alec fixes his gaze on the other me. Watching them makes my heart beat faster.

He says, "I want you to —" The video flickers out.

I stumble to the teeter-totter, but no one is there. Of course no one is there. I sit now where Alec sat looking at Lark. The virtual Alec and Lark. Ghosts.

I take a couple of breaths. What just happened? When my heart stops racing, I message Dad.

Lark:
On my way back to see you.
Need anything, Dad?

Dad:

I need you to stop worrying.

Nada más.

I'm fine. Go home.

Reid:

Are you home?

Wanted to talk to you.

As usual, failed.

Lark:

Sitting at the play park —

the one where you cut your head yrs ago.

Superweird thing just happened.

Reid:

Am still at Iona's.

Will meet you there.

Lark:

Good.

I lean back on the teeter-totter, which is hard along my spine. It creaks. I remember the day Reid cut his head open falling off the monkey bars when we were kids. I can picture us all, hear Nifty shrieking in this crazy high-pitched way that Iona teased him about for years, *"It's only blood."*

The evening is low and soft, and geese flock in a V-formation far above. I can make out faint honking. I imagine the flap of their wings, the connection between them that causes them to follow one another so perfectly. It makes me feel like the known world is only the edge of knowledge, that the depths are so much deeper than I can fathom. I remember being in grade one or two and feeling supersmart about something. I honestly thought I knew all the answers that day. But the answers are harder to find as I get older. I don't even know the right questions. Words to a song bubble into my mind. I reach for my cell to write, but another incoming message stops me:

He kisses me at the
base of my ear, and I'm melting,
helping him tug at my jeans.

Another video opens up. It's of me and Alec kissing on the teeter-totter. It's a looping video, very short, that replays again and again. From it, I hear myself sigh, as Alec slides his hand along my thigh.

The video flickers off.

Reid leans over me, his face framed against the growing night. "Uh, Lark, what's wrong? I mean ... everything okay?"

"I'm here, right?" I babble. "How could there be videos of me somewhere else? Well, not somewhere else, but here, with Alec? He's ... he's in a coma. He's not *here*."

Reid flops next to me, hunches his knees up and slides off his shoes, so his bare feet dip into the sandy ground. "What do you mean?"

I'm so relieved that he's taking me seriously that, for a second, I can't speak. He waits.

My phone pings:

Alec is on top of me.

His face is close to mine …

the weight of him …

I hold the screen up to Reid and say, "This keeps happening. Remember at Lydia's? I thought it was you sending me the messages."

"Lark, there's nothing on the screen."

I let out a cry of frustration. "But there was. Oh, God. What is happening?" The horrible thought comes to me that I'm going *insane.* Suddenly I can't breathe. "I've got to get out of here. I just need a little space to think."

"You're leaving?"

"I'm really sorry," I say. "I don't even know what I'm doing. Maybe I'm just overtired, I don't know."

"Hold on, Lark, let me help you figure this out."

I shake my head. "I'll message you later."

I pop into a corner store and pause against the drinks fridge to take a couple of breaths. I'm thinking about watching myself kiss Alec. *Alec is in a coma.* My head is spinning. And I just officially freaked out in front of Reid. Like, crazy-girl stuff. I mentally shake myself. Get a grip, Lark.

My gaze lands on a packet of chocolate-covered raisins. Mom used to love those. I'd forgotten, but we would take them to the hospital, and she'd put one in her mouth and let it dissolve on her tongue. Sometimes they made her throw up, but she still kept popping them in slowly, one by one.

I walk closer to the rack of candy and find myself slipping the crinkly bag into my backpack. It's larger than the other stuff I've stolen. The nail polish and the mascara were easy to disguise. I glance to see if there are cameras, still reassuring myself that I haven't done anything wrong. I could easily explain. There is a camera, but it's pointed toward the cash area, and the guy working the till is busy talking to a customer. I grab a second bag of chocolate-covered raisins and stuff them in my backpack with the first. Trembling, I take a couple of bags of chips from the shelf and walk over to pay for them. My mind calms, focusing. I smile at the guy, even flirt a little with my eyes. Part of me is asking myself what the hell I'm doing, but another part has this feeling of serenity, control.

I walk out smiling.

When I get back to the house, Lucy is sitting on the steps of the front porch, playing *Candy Crush*. She looks up from her phone and frowns.

"Uh, hey. Reid messaged saying you were losing it. I thought I'd stop by. What's up?"

"You know what, Lucy? Why don't we build up to my crazy. You tell me about you, then I'll tell you about me, okay?" I say.

"Deal." She cocks her head. "You know we were talking about me going away for a year? Well, it got me thinking. I've been doing a little research. What do you think about me starting in the UK, then heading to Paris?"

"Oooh, Paris — gotta be done."

"I'm actually excited about India, too. I read about it, and I'd love to go to a yoga retreat where I don't speak for eleven days. I know it's a long time until I go, but just thinking about it rocks."

"Eleven days? Not talking?" I give her a skeptical look.

She laughs.

I chuck her one of the bags of chocolate-covered raisins, which she catches. We sit together on the step. "That all sounds amazing. Tell me more. I could do with something other than me to focus on."

"You doing okay?"

"Maybe?"

I have an overpowering sense of déjà vu. This has happened before — but no. It's not something that's happened before. It feels like it's happening now ... but that makes no sense. The sensation trickles through my body like a small river. Maybe all my weird feelings are some sort of déjà vu. Like, a superintense version. But would that explain the videos and the messages?

I say to Lucy, "Déjà vu. That's a thing, right? The feeling that I've experienced something before?"

"Déjà vu is a thing. I think it's because we've all lived a past life. I was totally an Egyptian princess." Lucy gazes into the distance for a moment, then her eyes flick to me. "Why? Do you think you had a past life?"

A shudder goes through me. My surroundings start spinning.

We're quiet for a moment, and then she says, "You want to talk about it?"

"No. I don't know. It's ..." My voice trails off. I don't know if I can handle too much flaky stuff right now. When my mom was dying, people used to say dumb stuff like *Think positive. That will help.* Like it might. Or *"You need to fight this."* Like Mom wasn't. Or *"Have you tried eating more kale? Going to acupuncture? Reiki?"* Mom didn't resent people for being kind, but sometimes the wrong words made everything worse.

"Talk, already," she says.

"Okay," I say. "I'm dealing with some weird stuff."

"What sort of weird stuff?"

"It started with my phone. No. It started on the day that Alec nearly drowned."

"Tell me."

"I've been getting weird messages on my phone, and videos. Well, I think I'm getting them, but they always vanish. And I'm having ... hallucinations. Really strange."

"What do the messages say?"

"They talk about Alec. As if he's not in a coma. I wonder if I'm just wishing it were the case — maybe I'm imagining an alternative reality. Or maybe I've lived this whole life before. God, none of that makes sense at all."

"You're not exactly the sort of person to make this kind of thing up. Perhaps you're supersensitive to whatever's happening to you."

"But what do you think that is?"

She flips her hair over her shoulder. "I have no idea. I just think the world is more mysterious than we can possibly imagine."

"I think you're right."

In the quiet between us, I hear Suzanne's agonized cry.

Day 27: Saturday, early

I glance at my Tak on the wall. Mom gave it to me on my tenth birthday — it was way too big for me then. It was a gift for the future. Now it reminds me of everything she and I missed out on together. I turn away from the damn thing and look instead at the items on my bedside table.

This week I've stolen a memory stick, a gift card worth ten bucks and a box of Tic Tacs. Just little things, but I do it every day now, and the urge to keep the things has grown stronger — now I can't bear to throw them away like I did the mascara. I make sure to choose a different store every time, and I select parts of the store where there are no cameras. I can't even think about why I'm doing it. The bits and pieces are stacked next to the flowers that Annabelle's family gave me. I haven't yet thrown them away, although the water has long since evaporated and the petals are desiccated. I look at the calendar I've marked next to my bed. Alec's birthday will be day forty-five of his coma. I check off another day. He has just over two weeks left to live.

I fling myself out of bed. I have to get to work on time today, and I want a little time before I start at the café to catch up with Iona. I dress in a tunic and jeans with a blazer.

Dad was released from the hospital two days ago, but he's still exhausted. I'm worried they let him come home too soon, just because he wanted it so badly. I tiptoe past his room so as not to wake him, but he calls me to him. His face is still the same ashen gray.

"Off to work?"

I nod, going into his room and sitting on his bed. "But I didn't want to wake you."

"I'm pretty tired, actually." As he says this, he begins to drift off but then starts and wakes up again. "Oh, did you read the letter?"

I shake my head. "The letter?"

"Look in the dressing table. Maybe it's there." His voice is weak.

"A letter from Mom? Was it for my birthday?"

He nods, but his eyes drift shut, as if sleep is secretly stealing him without him even realizing it.

I get up from the bed and go to his wooden dressing table — the one that belonged to my mother — over by the window. Anything important he keeps there. The dresser was from Grams, and it's made of antique dark wood, with curly flowers etched into it. It's a girlie object for a man's bedroom, but there's no point saying anything to Dad.

I say it softly anyway, "You don't need to keep this, you know. It might be time to make it a bit more bacheloresque in here."

His eyes spring open, and for a heartbeat, he sounds like his old self. "*Bacheloresque* is not a word. Despite that, it's the last word I'll have from my daughter on the matter."

I pull a face. It's the same any time I try to suggest to him that it would be okay with me if he started dating. I truly think it would be. I'd like him to be with someone who loves him. But it's not a conversation we have. I reach into the drawer and discover a pile of envelopes.

"What are all these?"

"You put them back, Nosy-pops."

"I'm too old to be called 'Nosy-pops' anymore. They've got my name on them."

"Lark. I don't want you to look at those."

I have a flash of memories of when I was little. Mom laid out a treasure hunt for me around the house for each of my birthdays and clapped with delight when I worked out each clue. "I didn't know there were so many still for me to read. Why have I only had two so far? Was there one for my seventeenth? I wondered at the time."

"She wrote lots for you as an adult — one for your wedding, one for grad, other things. It was easier for her to write to you as an adult. Less painful." He looks out the window, his eyes blurring with tears. "She used any and every spare minute she had left to write to you. Oh, she had so much to say to you."

Sitting next to him on the bed, I remember my mother here in this room. Soft dark hair, a song, her lyrics.

He flips through the pile of letters I've handed him. "It's not here. I took it to the cemetery in case you met me there. It was in my shirt pocket."

"They cut that shirt off you, Dad, in the ER."

He looks stricken. "I'm sorry. I should have given it to you earlier. I can try and remember what she wrote." He yawns.

"Don't worry about it, Dad. Sleep. Rest," I say, though I ache to read words from my mom.

I hum to him and watch him fall asleep, my heart knotted. When I hear my phone, I hurry out of his room so it doesn't wake him. It's an email from the *Edenville Star*. They're sending someone to review the show! I whoop, then clap my hand over my mouth.

In the kitchen, while I chug back some coffee and eat half a bagel, I message Reid:

Lark:

I'm sorry for being so moody

and for kinda avoiding you.

Wanted to be the first to tell you —

I got the Edenville Star to come for the show!

Reid:

Sweet. You rock!

And no problem.

I text the rest of the band the good news. I've been working hard to publicize the event, ramping up the word on social media and trying to get people from the local press to commit. Focusing on this keeps me sane. I flick through my cell to see if there are any more weird messages or videos, but there aren't. There have been none since the message I tried to show Reid.

I zip up my knee-high boots and leave to meet Iona, pumped about the show.

Iona says when she sees me, "Nifty messaged. You have a new song ready for tomorrow's practice? And the *Star* is coming? You could have told me yourself."

"Oh, sure, because you were so easy to talk to earlier."

She sticks out her tongue. "Love the last song, by the way. And sweet news about the press. We rock. You rock." She blows me a kiss. "But I gotta go. Last-minute Roller Derby. Sorry —"

"I thought we were having coffee!"

"Another time!" She blows me another kiss.

I imagine the kiss flying toward me and landing on my cheek. Something in it makes me feel ready. I can do this. *Seize the day.* I message Reid:

Lark:

Gotta work in an hour.

Wanna come with me to Fields Studios?

We could drop in,

tell the receptionist about the show ...

Reid:

Meet you there.

When we get to the studio, I pause at the glass doors. The frontage is almost all glass, and through the back, I glimpse the river. Fields Studios is about as good as it gets for hundreds of miles. They've got a great online presence and a cool radio show and a cult following all over the country. I look up and imagine myself recording here. Our school took a class trip here when we were in grade four, and I remember feeling like I'd come home. The technician let me be the kid who sang in the actual studio. Mom was so delighted. It thrilled me for years.

Reid says, "So *the* Martin Fields is the father of the girl you saved. And he gave you his card ages ago. And you kept that to yourself."

He narrows his eyes at me behind his glasses.

"This is the sort of thing that you'll get interviewed about one day."

I pretend to be holding a mic. "Yeah. I worked for his family, hoping to meet him one day. But it was the day I saved his kid's life when it all changed —" Even as I goof off, I think of Alec in his coma. What if I'd saved him instead?

The doors open automatically, and we're met with air-conditioning and the smell of cleaning products. Inside it's crisp and shiny, with white walls and a huge red sign that reads FIELDS STUDIOS alongside posters of singers, most of them signed. The receptionist has about a million tattoos, even a tangled tree growing up her neck over her right cheek and scalp. Her white-blond hair is shaved on one side, and she's gorgeous. Reid shuffles uncomfortably next to me, totally tongue-tied by the hot girl.

"I'm here to drop off an invite for Martin Fields." I try to sound confident and not like a hopeful loser.

"He's just in the back," the gorgeous girl says. "Do you want to give it to him personally? I find that helps. He can't always come to these things, but we might as well try, right?" She smiles conspiratorially with us.

If I ever do get interviewed about how I started out, she's totally going to be in the story.

Reid says, "I dunno if we should disturb —"

I jab him in the ribs. "Could you, um, please tell him that Lark —"

At that moment a white door opens, and Martin comes in. He's got large headphones on, but when he sees us, he takes them off and slides his cell into the pocket of his hoodie. The door shuts behind him.

He rubs his thumb across his stubble and says, "Lark. Great to see you. What's that?"

"I don't want to pressure you." I pass him the printout I made online last night. It's a simple flyer showing our name and the time we perform.

He holds up one finger and waves it side to side. "Not the way to start. Let me give you a tip. When you approach an exec, you need to be confident."

I try again, reaching out so he drops his raised hand to shake mine. I say, "You should come to this."

"Better. Why?"

"Because you'll like our sound." I glance at Reid. "Right?"

Martin, who is studying the flyer, says without looking up, "Confidence, Lark, confidence."

"You would. We're good. Indie, mellow but edgy, musical, not prepackaged."

"I'll come," he says, looking up. "'Saturday Drowning'?"

There is a moment of quiet between us. I'm sure he's thinking about what could have happened that day. And I'm thinking about Alec. *Lark! DO SOMETHING!*

"Next time," Martin says, "give a little more warning."

"Right," I say. *Two weeks isn't enough warning?* I'm smiling hard. He's going to come! This is mind-blowingly awesome. "I will." Then the white door he has just come through gives a strange creak. I turn toward it as it groans and the very fabric of it strains.

Water seeps from underneath the door, pooling quickly toward us. A flickering in the air by the door reveals what looks like a screen suspended in the air; the image on it is the hospital room I saw before. Annabelle lying small and silent in a too-big hospital bed. Dead flowers everywhere. Below the bed — either in the studio where I stand or in the hospital room, it's impossible to tell — water is spreading over the floor. It is muddied, and small leaves and plants are washed along in the flow.

Suddenly in the flickering screen, I see a face. It's another girl, her long black hair trailing like seaweed, her eyes wide with horror. As I recognize her, my own eyes widen, too.

She's *me.*

The water reaches my shoes — wet and freezing. It shocks me back to the studio where I'm standing, Martin and Reid frowning at me. Stark fear threatens to drown me.

Chapter Five
Chapter Five

Day 32: Thursday, after school

When I get home from school, Dad tells me he's going out for supper and then to see John Fogerty.

"Without me?" I say.

"You hardly know his stuff. I'm going with, uh, friends."

"And what am I supposed to do?"

"Lark, you're a teenager. Go out."

"But you're not one hundred percent."

That merits a mock glare from him.

After he leaves, I try to find something to do with my evening. I was supposed to be working, but Tish gave my shift to someone else, apologizing for the mix-up. I've seen her do that to other staff before … as she's figuring out how to fire them. I don't want to lose the job, but there's nothing I can do about it. I eat a sandwich and watch TV for ages.

Discovering that all my so-called friends are too busy even to reply to a message, and that Alec's at work for a little longer, I go back to the song lyrics my mom left. I stare at them and then put them to a little music to see if I can make them work. As I sing, a couple of the lines stand out. The words are like exclamation marks:

"Parallel you
Parallel me
Just the way it needs to be
You, me, if only …"

I stop singing, my throat dry. Then I sing the words to myself again, slowly. Oh, my God. Perhaps *this* explains what happened when I saw Annabelle.

Lark:
Can you come over?
Urgent …

Alec:
Sure. Just finishing up.

Alec stops at my house on his way home.

"What's up?" he asks, as I take him up to my room. He kisses me and flops into my desk chair.

"Listen to this." I sing him the lines over.

"Nice. You wrote a song?"

"I wish. These are words from Mom. I was trying to add a melody, so I'd have something for the band tomorrow. I've really got nothing for them. Anyway, as I was singing it, well, I know it sounds crazy, but …"

"What?"

I pass him the page and jab the words with my finger.

Parallel you
Parallel me
Just the way it needs to be
You, me, if only ...

I open my hands to him. "What if that's it?"

"What?"

"Isn't it obvious?"

First confusion washes over his face, then sympathy. I don't want sympathy. I explain, "It's not PTSD — I'm telling you, it's real. What if this is it? *Parallel* lives — look at what she's written there. If we each have another life, wouldn't that explain what I saw when we were at the hospital?"

He bites his bottom lip.

"Alec, if there are parallel lives, what's going on with us in the other one?"

He tries a joke. "Maybe we're making out instead of talking about pseudoscience?" When I don't laugh, he pushes a strand of hair back from my face and looks at me earnestly. "Don't you think this is just some sort of reaction to what happened with us at the lake that day? Not to mention all the stuff with your dad. Remember how you only freak out at the hospital?"

"What about the messages?"

"I don't know what to say. I haven't ever seen one, remember?"

I bury my head in my hands and groan. "I can't figure out what it all means."

"Tell me about it."

"It's possible, isn't it? What if these lyrics mean that Mom lived a parallel life, too? Maybe she knew."

"Lark, this is a mishmash of … well, I mean, first you're living a parallel life, then your mom is?"

"What about the video on my phone? It all makes sense now."

"Okay, Lark. Honestly? Parallel lives? These are just lyrics." He tosses the papers lightly to the floor.

"Don't do that," I say, more loudly than I had intended. I sink to my knees and scramble for the pages.

He holds up his hands, palms facing me.

"Sorry, Lark, I don't want to be a jerk … but I don't know if … I didn't sign up for this."

"Sign up for what?"

"This —"

He gestures toward me on my knees, gripping the sheets of paper.

"This is important to me," I say.

"I get that." His jaw is clenched. "I actually have to go. My mom needs me for something tonight."

"What? You're leaving?"

"It's not just you and all this …"

He points at the sheets of paper in my hands.

"It's things at home."

What am I doing? I put Mom's notes on my bed and pull myself to my feet. "Talk to me."

"I will. Just not now. Okay?"

We stare at each other for a long moment.

"Okay?" he repeats.

"I guess so."

He stands and kisses me gently, and then a little harder.

"First, can we stop all this parallel lives, or whatever it is, stuff?"

"I'm sorry." I swallow my rising resolve to understand all this. "I'll drop it."

Though I keep worrying about what's going on with Alec at home, there's one thought that keeps flashing. Parallel lives could explain all this. I remember the video of Reid that I saw at the play park — what else could it be but footage from my parallel life? But how did it get to my cell?

I spend some time online looking up the words *parallel lives*. Most of what I find is flaky, but it speaks to me. Two lives at the same time. I wonder why this would be happening to me — I can almost sense a second version of myself, close but far away.

My heart sputters. My mom is dead in this life. But what if she's alive in another life? A parallel one?

I look over the words:

In the dream
I shifted
Between finding
The portal showed me
How to
Go through
You have to trust me
You have to go
Back to the beginning
Jump
End it

To break
And resolve
I'm so
Sorry, baby.

The word *portal* stands out. A portal — a doorway. To what? Another life? A way through. I hold up my cell — could it be the portal? I flick from screen to screen. I read some parallel-life stuff on the internet. I type in the word *portal*. A bunch of sites come up, but none of them seem to connect to me and my experience.

I rub my eyes. I'm tired. I should just go to bed. But instead I read the song again, as if it were true, as if it were a clue. *Back to the beginning.* Well, that was the day of the near drowning of Alec.

My brain leaps to Annabelle. How both times I went to see her, I had a hallucination. But what if they *weren't* hallucinations? Could they instead have been glimpses of my other life? I think about what that life might be like — better than this one? Worse? Oh, God, what if in the other life something worse has happened to Annabelle? Do I want to know? I feel like I'm falling, with no one to catch me. Who am I in that life? How can I get there? Do I even want to get there?

Dolphin:
Are you coming over?

Lark:
Sorry! Forgot.
On my way.

I slip out and away. The air is freezing, the clouds and drizzle from earlier replaced by a clear, bitter night. I get to Dolphin and Lucy's quickly. The house is impeccably tidy from the outside. I have a flash of myself aged about seven, sitting in this yard on a checked blanket with Lucy, staring up at this crabapple tree.

Lark:
I'm here.

Dolphin:
Come on in.

Dolphin opens the door. She has her hair in braids like Lucy's, but hers are streaked with gray.

"So what's going on — I mean, it's nice to see you, but why without Lucy around?" Dolphin has always been direct: she's not a small-talk person.

"I can explain. Thanks for letting me come over."

"Anytime. You know you haven't been here very much since … oh, Lark, you … it's just … I mean, you look just like her. Your hair is just like hers."

She blinks back tears, reaches to lift a long black strand away from my face, and then we are hugging. I imagine Mom already on her way inside, about to put on coffee.

Dolphin leads me into her living room. It's as messy as always. Tidy outside, chaos inside. Stacks of papers piled up everywhere. Books scattered over the carpet. Two kittens tumble over each other, darting around the houseplants. The house smells of cat pee, of soil from the plants, of dust. One of Lucy's painting hangs above the mantel — it's of a huge spiral.

An image comes to mind of my mother sitting on this couch, laughing, her feet curled underneath her.

Whenever I come here with Lucy, we use the side door and make our way down to her room in the basement. Coming through the front door makes me feel differently about this house. It hurts to be in this room where my mom spent so much time. I decide to settle where she used to sit, but to do so, I have to move a pile of magazines to the floor.

Dolphin hands me hot chocolate and a plate of muffins. "You want one of these?"

I accept one and take a bite. The muffin tastes of bananas, honey, oats, the past. "Yum."

"So," she says, sitting in her favorite armchair. "Much as I love having you here, what's up?"

"Okay." I pull out the song lyrics.

She sits quietly as I read the lyrics to her, and the letter.

"You maybe knew her best. Is there anything you remember about this song?" I ask.

"In what way?"

"Can you tell me first? Then I'll explain."

Dolphin takes the papers. "It's so nice to hear one of her songs again — I mean, I know it's not fully formed or anything," she murmurs. "It makes me think of a conversation we had once. See, your mom was a pretty amazing woman. She was rooted in reality, in the solid things of life, but she had this other side to her — her artistic side, her nature, her being. She could cook supper for you and your dad and then curl up with a pen and write the most gorgeous song. It's that side of her that connected with me, I think. I mean, we were so different. But I believed her. See, she believed in parallel lives — really believed in them. She dreamed about them all the time."

"She did?" I put my muffin down on a small plate and lean forward.

"This was a long time before she got sick. She talked to your dad about it, but I don't know that he really got it. Your mom ... this is going to sound crazy, but her dreams were so vivid that she believed they were glimpses of her other possible life. Then, when she was running out of time, she mentioned it again, often. I suspect that's when she was trying to write this song. Having a parallel life was something that she longed for when she was dying — a life where she got to see you growing up."

"Nothing else?"

"Like what?"

"Like, did she say she lived a parallel life?"

Dolphin looks at me for a long time. "Like I said, I think being diagnosed made her wish for one — it was her thing. You know ... artistically, it spoke to her. Every artist has a theme. Parallel lives was hers."

"So, she might have done it? I mean, she might have lived a parallel life and been aware of it — and that's why she wrote this song?"

"That's not what she said to me. Look, I don't want to speak out of turn here, but she and your dad argued about it. He wanted her to be in the here and now, not longing for whatever wasn't possible. He was afraid it would give you, Lark, false hope."

Tears spring to my eyes. A question has been forming at the back of my mind. I have to turn my hopes into spoken words. "The thing is, do you think ... if there's such a thing as alternate lives ... Do you think my mother's alive in another life now?"

"Lark …"

"I mean, there might be a parallel life where she's okay. Right? Where she never got sick. Do you think I might get to see her again?"

For a moment, Dolphin doesn't speak. But her face turns white. "Oh, Lark. I'm so sorry. I should have realized … oh, this is what your father wanted to avoid."

"No. No. I'm not making it up. The parallel-life stuff."

"Your mom was a creative person. Look. I mean, I know I have Witches' Brew, and I do believe there are other ways to understand the world. We don't have all the answers, Lark, but you have to understand the nuances. A parallel life? It exists. But I believe your dad was right. It's on a metaphorical plane, honey. It's a way to experience life, this one. And the other life? Well, that's a dream, a story, a song … We are all living other possible lives, but we can ONLY be in one life, and if we spend our time hoping and dreaming for the life we aren't living, we suffer. I didn't mean that your mom is alive. You can't go and see her. That's not healthy for you to hope for. I'm so sorry, sweet pea."

It's been a long time since anyone called me "sweet pea." It was what my mother called me. Something inside me cracks, like ice on the river after a long winter. Tears slide down my cheeks, and Dolphin comes to give me a hug. I let her hold me while I cry and cry.

Day 38: morning

I push aside a pile of clothes and haul myself out of bed. I check on Dad, but he's already up, and when I get to the kitchen, he's made coffee. I perch on the counter stool and take a cup gratefully. I stir in three sugars, and Dad clucks his tongue with disapproval.

We sit in silence for a few moments.

He lets out a long breath. "Dolphin called me last night."

Uh-oh, here it comes.

"She said you visited her a few days ago. She said you were talking about some pretty intense stuff. And apparently Lucy said you've been a little cool with her. Dolphin didn't want to intrude, but she felt she had to call me — she's worried about you. Basically."

"It's nothing. I was talking to Dolphin about some stuff."

"Right. Care to elaborate?"

"She's obviously told you already."

"Your mom was very sick at the end. Lark, she was hopeful. She didn't want to leave you."

"What if she was telling the truth? What if it's real?"

Dad slams his hand on the table. Hard. It makes us both jump.

"What if it *were* real? What difference does it make to either of us?"

He lets out a shuddering breath, and I can tell he's trying not to cry. When he speaks again, he changes the subject.

"What's up with you and Lucy?"

"We're fine," I say woodenly. "Nothing's wrong."

"Lark ..."

Alec:

How's it going, baby?

Lark:

S'okay. Just talking to Dad.

Are you feeling better?

Wanna meet b4 school if you're coming in?

Alec:

I can't.

He missed school because he was ill most of last week, but he refused to let me visit. I thought he'd be back yesterday, but he still didn't show. I miss him so much it hurts.

Lark:

Anywhere. Want to see you.

I'm a good nurse ;-)

Alec:

I bet.

I'll call you later.

Lark:

Seriously.

Is everything okay?

You've been sick forever.

"Lark — I should take that cell phone away from you." Dad finishes his coffee and goes to wash out the cup in the sink.

"Should I be worried about you?"

"I'm … I'll be fine."

He seems like he's about to say something else, but I'm distracted again:

Alec:

I'll be back at school tomorrow.

I gotta go xxx

By the time I've read it, Dad is on his way toward the door. "Next time we talk, put the phone away. I have to go to work. Have a good day at school."

Alec:

Actually, plan B.

Cut school with me.

We'll go climbing.

I don't even hesitate.

Lark:

Yes.

Alec:

Xxx

The weather is growing colder by the day, now that we're fully into October. We still have a while until the snow falls, but in the brisk wind there's a hint of what's coming. Alec waits for me in the play park. He has a bruise on his cheek, faded but obvious.

"What's that?" I ask.

He gets up and wraps his arms around me.

"Alec, my God. Are you okay?"

"Can we just go climbing?"

"I'm your girlfriend, right?"

He nods.

"So talk to me."

But he is silent. He holds my hand and won't catch my eye.

We walk together quietly. At the back of the park is a disused house with signs around it saying not to go past the wire fencing. Alec squeezes through a large gap in the fence. After checking over each shoulder, I follow him.

"Is it safe?"

He ignores me and starts to climb.

I make sure my cell is tucked deep into my pocket, and then I climb after him. I call up, "Does the fear ever go away?"

He glances down. "Definitely. But then you just do something scarier … *bwa-ha-ha-ha.*"

At his teasing, the fear I've been feeling shifts up through my body and bursts out the top of my head, to be replaced by glee.

Quickly we reach the roof. He helps me stand. I'm here. Yet at the same time, I feel completely disconnected from myself, as if I'm both inside my own body and outside it. I haul myself back to reality. Right now, I'm standing at the top of a building. Alec is next to me, and we're laughing about something. Though I have no idea what. I wobble, and he grabs me. He turns to me, his eyes serious.

"Thank you. For not asking a bunch of questions."

I'm desperate for him to tell me what's going on, and my guesses make me afraid for him. But I say, "I get it. When my mom was sick, I didn't want to talk all the time. But holding it inside isn't good, you know? I do want you to talk to me — at some point."

"I will. I promise."

We stand there for a long time. Up here, the air is cool, and there is so much sky.

His eyes focus on mine. "I know this comes out of nowhere," he says. "I know I've been distant. But I have to tell you something." He puts his hand under my shirt at the waist, his palm warm on my stomach. "I've never said this to a girl before ... but I love you, Lark. I do."

My insides vault. He loves me, he loves me. I have everything I want. Then a dark thought appears, a cloud on the horizon of my mind. I've been trying to believe Dolphin and to put the thought of parallel lives aside, but now a possible parallel life suddenly frightens me. Is Alec with me in my parallel life? Does he love me like this?

Or is he the one in the coma instead of Annabelle?

I plunge from the heights of joy to fear.

"Are you going to say anything?" he asks.

"Sorry. I was just ..."

His hurt expression stops me. I need to be in the moment. "I love you, too," I say.

We spend a long time kissing before we leave our spot close to the sun.

Dad is out at work for the day, so Alec and I go to my house.

We hunt through the pantry, both of us starving. We find some frozen ground beef, so I defrost it in the microwave while I search through my mom's old recipe book for a dessert. I settle on her favorite: blackstrap molasses cake. Alec hangs out, watching a movie.

"Lark, stop cooking," he calls. "I'd be happy with a sandwich."

"No, this is going to be good," I say. "Worth the wait." I let the words hang. I realize I'm ready.

"Oh, crap," he says, looking at his phone. "I gotta go. My mom ..."

"But I was going to feed you and then seduce you."

"I told you not to waste time on the feeding part." He kisses me. "Sorry, I gotta go."

"Is your mom okay?" I'm not surprised when he shrugs off my question. And I don't probe, even though I want to.

"Save me some cake."

We kiss goodbye. Then I stir the molasses with eggs, flour and sugar, remembering how Mom used to do the same thing. I add ginger and cinnamon, and their spicy warmth fills the kitchen. As for the beef, Mom taught me to cook it for a long time, browning it for flavor, so I put it in a pan on the stovetop and begin the slow stir, thinking again about my alternate life. I miss Lucy — I bet she'd have interesting things to say about all this. It's not that we're not speaking. More that we're just cool with each other. Polite. And I haven't hung out with the band for ages.

To my surprise, tears spill from my eyes. I wipe them away. I stir the meat and add a little boiling water to help the browned edges blend. It smells good, rich and filling. I search for my cell. Hanging out with Alec, I forgot about it. I find it at the bottom of my pocket. There are hardly any messages, as if I'm slowly vanishing from my own life.

I reply to Nifty, who is asking if I'm coming to rehearsal, telling him of course and asking how he is. He's been in a bad mood since he broke up with Cole the other week, but I'm still surprised when he doesn't respond. I check my work schedule online. I only have a Saturday-night shift this entire week. Alec has messaged a couple of times since he left. I try to imagine him in a coma — what would life be like without him? I Google "comas." Nothing I read is good. Annabelle might never recover. She could be in a coma for years, if the doctors don't recommend ending her life support. My inner voice whispers, *You should go and see Annabelle. Go now.*

I push the suggestion away. I'm not doing that. It feels so wrong to torture a little girl and her mother just to find out answers, to find myself in my other life and see if I can figure this out. But how can I not try to see if I am living two lives? What if I go and find out something terrible — what if I go and find out it's not real? Would that lift this *feeling* from me?

The oven beeps. I take out the cake, glad of the distraction from my own head. I pour tomatoes over the beef and put a lid on the casserole dish, and then I place the whole thing in the oven.

Dad:
I won't be home for supper.

Lark:
I'm making Bolognese sauce.
I'll leave it out.

Heat it up with some pasta.

Xxx

Dad:

LU xxx

Lark:

Me too xoxo

I spend a while watching bad TV and eating. I glance over some of my old songs, trying to get ready for practice, realizing that I'm nervous about going. I reassure myself it'll be fine, it's only my band, but I've skipped a bunch of practices, and I know they're mad that I'm not ready for the show.

If only there were some other way to figure out this parallel life stuff. My brain ticks through possibilities again. When I've seen Annabelle in the hospital, I've been able to see what may be my parallel life. I replay the same argument: it's ghoulish to visit a kid in a coma to get something for myself. Maybe I don't have to be with Annabelle physically — maybe just thinking about Annabelle will get me there. I focus on Annabelle's image in my mind, her small body in the bed. I see her vividly in my head now. Her pale face. The beep of the heart monitors. But it's not working. As if it would. Dolphin is probably right. None of this is real.

I sigh and give up. I resolve instead to work really hard tonight to write a song. At practice I'll show them what I've got; that'll get me back on an even keel with them. And I plan to fix things with Lucy, too.

But I'm exhausted at the prospect of trying to do any of this.

I lean back into the couch and close my eyes. I'll do all of it later, after I've caught up on some sleep.

Day 41: too early

Since I slept through band practice three days ago, the band has been furious with me. So I told them there was no way I was doing their stupid show with them. It was just one practice. I hoped they might care even a little bit that I was quitting, but if anything, they seemed relieved. Perhaps I was relieved, too. But now none of them are talking to me. I don't care. It's becoming clearer and clearer that the only person who is there for me is Alec.

We spent yesterday evening hiking along the river trails. He taught me how to do a better wall jump. My hands are still sore from trying to pull myself up, but I've got a better technique now. Afterward we watched a bunch of stuff at his house about parkour, wishing his mom would leave, but she didn't.

I dress in my pastel jeans with the hole and a black T-shirt with a low back. I sling on a lacy sweater and spend a little time putting on mascara and giving myself smoky eyes.

I grab my longboard and take it outside. It's raining lightly, the day gray and cool but refreshing. I wonder what she's doing now. The other me. Is she getting on her longboard, too? Is she going to visit Alec in the hospital, where he's in a coma? I check my cell. No messages, nothing. I argue with myself yet again. I was wrong about all this. Perhaps Dolphin was right.

For the thousandth time, my inner voice tells me to go and see Annabelle. Prove this to myself once and for all. I have to stop waiting at the sidelines of my life. I have to figure this out.

Poor Alec.
They turn off the life support
in four days ...

It's the first message I've had for days. As it vanishes, I start to tremble. It feels like some sort of sick joke, but what if it's true, and they're really switching off his life support? Alec can't die. *Not in any life.* No. I know what I have to do. I have to go and see Annabelle. I have to find the truth.

I hurry to the hospital, listening on the way to some terrible pop playlist. I lean my board against a wall and enter through the main doors. The hallway is full of other people, wrapped up in their own lives, dealing with life and death.

Alec:
Where are you?
Can we talk?

Lark:
Not now.

Alec:
Playing hard to get? ;-)

Lark:
Come by later.

Alec:
B over at 7.

I realize I've already reached the third floor when the elevator dings and the doors slide open. I pad toward Pediatrics to see Annabelle. The rest of my plan is kind of fuzzy.

I'm reaching to push open one of the double doors, when a sign pulls me up short:

VISITORS RESTRICTED

After a surge in respiratory illnesses, the health region is restricting visitors to the Pediatric and Pediatric Intensive Care Wards to PARENTS ONLY.

I read it over three times and slam the wall with my fist. Then I open one of the double doors and peek around to see if anyone has noticed me.

I get five steps along the hallway before a nurse approaches, frowning.

"Excuse me, who are you here to see?"

"Uh, um, Annabelle Fields."

Politely but firmly, the nurse moves in front of me. "Did you see the sign?"

"Uh, no," I lie.

"You'll have to wait to visit. We have restrictions on visitors. You don't want to make anyone sick, do you?"

There's nothing to do about the situation. I shake my head and mumble an apology. Then I hurry away. My hand hurts from slamming it into the wall. I rub it all the way out of the hospital. After all that, I can't see Annabelle?

I board home. Dad's not there. I boil some water and eat a Pot Noodle in front of the TV. When the doorbell rings, I go to it gratefully.

"I'm so glad to see you," I say, as Alec wraps me up in his

arms. At least now I can forget about Annabelle. "Do you want to come to my room?"

He is kissing me and nodding at the same time. It feels so right. I don't want him to stop. Not now. Not ever. I pull him upstairs.

"Are you ready?" He pulls off my black T-shirt.

I peel off my pastel jeans. "I'm ready."

Dad calls from downstairs, "Lark, are you home?"

Alec groans as I pull my jeans back up. "This is never going to happen," he says. "I should just go."

"I'm up here, Dad," I call back. I stick my tongue out at Alec.

We go downstairs to chat with Dad for a few moments and then outside, me with my longboard. Alec gets a call from a parkour friend, and I tell him I'll meet him under the bridge in a while. It's just occurred to me that perhaps there's a way to get to Annabelle after all.

I longboard back to the hospital. I've worked out how to do this; I just need to make sure I don't get caught. I slide my longboard into the bushes along the back wall of the hospital and spend a few minutes figuring out which window is Annabelle's. The pathway is empty, and though there's traffic going by, I'm going to guess that most people are too preoccupied with their own lives to notice me.

After checking that no one is watching, I begin to climb. I've made it to the second floor, when I see a couple walking below. They stop right beneath me, and the woman fumbles for her phone. She shows him something on the screen, while I press against the rough brick wall, hardly breathing. Finally they walk on, and I make it to the third floor, my muscles aching and shaky.

I shimmy along to the window I guessed to be Annabelle's. Another child is in the bed. A small boy. My eyes fill with tears. What am I doing? I'm losing my mind. A nurse comes into the room, and I watch quietly and wait. After she leaves, the boy turns toward the door. I pass the window as quickly as I can and try the next one along. It's another child, again not Annabelle but an older girl, chatting with her mom. I can't go by their window. They'll spot me. I duck out of sight, sweating and desperately trying to understand how to find Annabelle's room. I look along the row of windows and count. It doesn't help. I'm never going to find her. I shimmy back to the window where the boy is. I'm about to give up and go back down, when I think of how badly I need to understand this. So I keep going past the boy's room to the next window in that direction.

This time I've got it right. It's Annabelle. She lies there, still as the grave, and alone. Suzanne is out of the room — a lucky break.

But the window is closed. I wonder suddenly if it's even possible to open the window, and my body begins to sweat — a prickly sweat. If I get caught here, if I fall, if I … I steady my breathing and fumble around with the window. To my surprise, it opens easily, and I slide in.

I hurry to Annabelle, and before I can think too much more about it, I sit by her and lightly touch her hand.

From where I stand, the window frames the sky, but as I look at it, the glass begins to crack. Tiny fracture lines spread like tree branches, and to my horror, they extend up into the white ceiling.

And water is seeping in. Rapidly it goes from a trickle to a flood, rising from the floor; the walls are pushed outward by the force of it. I open my mouth, but water pours in, making me gag.

Soon I'm underwater, fighting to keep my head above the surface, fighting for air. And there is the flickering screen, and through it the other Lark is there, too, frantically struggling to keep her head above water. *I knew. I knew. I knew.*

I swim toward the screen, toward her. I feel like I might die, the effort is so immense. But then, with a ripping feeling through my entire body, as if my insides are being torn from me, I'm there.

I'm standing on my street, looking at myself. Oh, my God.

She's me. She's wearing the same jeans, the same shirt, the same everything. Even the same makeup. But her hair only just reaches into a ponytail and is dyed red.

"Can you hear me?" I say to her. To myself.

"Oh, my God. I can hear you," she replies.

Chapter Six

Chapter Six

Day 32: after school

Lucy and I walk to work together on Thursday. She looks like she's wearing a rainbow sheep — her secondhand wool coat is a multitude of colors. We chat about the show. I pull my coat around me to keep out the cool drizzle. I'm wearing one earbud and listening to "Werewolves of London" while we walk, drifting into my own thoughts in that comfortable way that happens between good friends.

Lucy twinkles at me. "So, you and Reid?"

"What?" Then I laugh. "Me and Reid? Come on, Lucy. That's ridiculous."

"You told me he asked you on a date at practice that one time."

I push open the door to D'Lish. "Yeah, I'm pretty sure that was as friends."

She gives me a funny smile. "If you say so."

We're enveloped in warmth and noise and the smell of coffee. "I say so." I take off my coat and pass a cluster of people having a lively meeting.

As we enter the kitchen, she puts on her black apron. I hang my coat up, grab my apron and knot my hair into a braid.

Our manager glares at us. "Hurry up. I need someone on the counter."

When her back is turned, I pull a face.

Lucy whispers, "You and Reid are totally making out."

"I'm going to help at the front," I say, shimmying past her. "You get cleanup."

She sticks her tongue out at me.

Nifty comes to meet us when we finish work. It's almost midnight. He presses his face against the window like a puppy. When we open the door, he almost falls inside the café.

"Give me warmth," he moans. He's wearing superskinny pants and a ripped tee with only a linen jacket. He vapes and dances foot to foot.

"Put some clothes on," I say. "And get out of here with that. No smoking." I close the door and lock it. "Seriously, Nifty, you need to wear more."

Lucy, who is snuggled into her sheep coat, bleats, "Like me-e-e-e-e."

"Indeed. Look at this fine example of warmth and fashion." I gesture at her.

Nifty laughs.

"This, you poor fools, isn't about fashion. It's about respect for the planet. I'm reusing. Recycling," Lucy says.

Nifty laughs. "You are most definitely doing that."

He puts an arm around her, and we stroll out into the freezing night.

As the three of us walk toward my house, I say, "So, Nifty, what's going on with you and Cole? I haven't heard anything since your supper."

"Did she give you advice?" Lucy asks. "Never, ever listen to her advice."

Nifty says, "His parents loved me."

"Really?'

"Well, they didn't hate me. Cole and I are perhaps working on it." He pumps his pelvis.

"Good," I say. "I think."

"Oh, it's goo-o-o-o-o-d," says Nifty.

"I get it, thanks. Is he coming to the show?" I ask.

Nifty shrugs and looks at Lucy. In the streetlight, I make out his expression. It's half eye roll, half smile. "She's obsessed. The show, the show, the show."

"Aren't you?" I ask.

We arrive at my house and go up the back steps. The lights are out. I panic — there's no way Dad is well enough to be out anywhere. I text him five times.

Dad:
Just went for a walk.
Relax. I'm okay.

I follow the others to the den. Nifty picks a movie. About half an hour into it, Dad sticks his head around the door.

"You kids okay?"

"Where were you?"

He doesn't answer. "Lucy, is that magnificent beast in the mud room something to do with you?"

She beams. "That, Vince, is my coat."

"Fantastic," he says. "I was out, my lovely Lark."

"Dad, have you been drinking? You said you went for a walk."

He winks. "Maybe a glass or two. Now, enough questions. This old man needs to go to bed."

"What about your heart?"

"Really, it was only a glass and a half. Don't worry, baby. I'm just —" he grins again "— in a good mood. 'Night." And with that, he's gone back upstairs.

I look at my friends. "What was that about?"

"I might not be the only one having a goo-o-o-o-o-d time," Nifty says.

I throw a pillow at him. "Ew. He's only just got out of hospital. He's not having sex, Nifty. Gross."

We turn our attention back to the movie, and I realize I haven't thought about anything except the present moment for hours.

Day 38: dawn

I roll over in bed and check my cell:

M. Fields:
I'll be there on the 31st.
Listened to your band online.
Been meaning to.
You guys are good.
I mean that.

Lark:
Thanks

M. Fields:
See you v soon.

It's horribly early, but there's no way I can go back to sleep after reading that. I haul myself out of bed, push aside a pile of clothes and slip on a black shirtdress, which I belt with a checked scarf. I read over the song lyrics I've been working on:

A moment in pieces
Take a shard of me
Look deeply inside for remnants
of how we used to be
Part the water, slide in a ripple
Find yourself in time
Find me.

A tiny sliver enters
Turns my heart to ice
Shows me the way our life could be
Could be
Part the water, slide in a ripple
Find yourself in time
Find me.

I'm Gretel in a picture book
And you're leaving me
If I turn the pages, I sense
We could live a different story
Part the water, slide in a ripple
Find yourself in time
Find me.

A thousand hours in a moment
A million lifetimes that could have been
If I'd stayed dressed on the shore
Made you see the way back to me
The screwed-up life of you and me.

The reflective shattered pieces
Show me the way our life could be
Part the water, slide in a ripple
Find yourself in time
Find me
Find me
Find me.

I reread the line about Gretel. I check online and realize that I'm talking about the wrong fairy tale. It's "The Snow Queen" that has a character with a shard of glass entering her heart, turning it to ice. I sing it out loud anyway, to see if it matters, but I decide the whole verse is messy. I rework it.

I look at my Tak. I want to take it down and try the song with it. I might be able to figure out the messed-up verse. My hands shake slightly. Instead I pull out Iona's guitar and spend an hour with the melody I worked out with Nifty. We've been sending each other stuff, and the song is really coming together. The verse remains all wrong, but I decide not to worry about it. I play it again and find myself changing a note here and there.

Eventually my body demands caffeine. Before I leave my room, I mark another day on the calendar I have for Alec. He has only seven days before the machines are turned off. Seven pathetic days, and if only I'd saved him, he might be here now instead.

I check on Dad, but he's already up, and when I get to the kitchen, he's made coffee. I perch on the counter stool and take a cup gratefully. I stir in three sugars, and Dad clucks his tongue in disapproval.

I show him the text from Martin, and he punches me lightly on the shoulder. "Your mom would be so proud."

"Thanks."

He pulls lightly on his bottom lip. "So, yeah, I've been thinking."

"What? This sounds serious. Thinking's bad for the brain, remember?"

He ruffles my hair, and I immediately smooth it.

"I — uh — maybe met someone ..."

"Okay ... where?"

"She's a volunteer at the hospital."

I ease off the stool to hug him. "That's great, Dad. Really great. What's her name?"

"Alyssa. She's ... she's nice. But I'm doing it for you," he says. "You don't want to be looking after your old dad anymore."

"Ah, so you're looking for a nurse? Not a date?"

"Cheeky." He grins. "Though I probably should make it clear to her that I'm not looking for a nurse. She's actually a teacher. She spends Saturdays at the hospital ..." He finishes his coffee and goes to wash out the cup in the sink.

I sip my hot, sugary coffee.

Suddenly his shoulders hunch, as if he's in pain.

"Are you okay, Dad?" I ask. "What did you eat for breakfast?"

"See?" he says, brushing off my concern, turning to face me and smiling. "I definitely need a girlfriend, not a daughter who's turning into my mother." He waves and ducks out the door.

I call after him, "You need to eat!"

Reid:
Wanna ride to school?

Lark:
Sure.

Lucy:
You awake?

Lark:
Been up forever.

Me and Me

Lucy:

Wanna get me eight tickets for the show?

Lark:

Eight? Sweet.

Lucy:

My cousins are coming to town.

And parents want to come. Okay?

Lark:

Come over.

Reid giving me a ride.

Lucy:

I bet he is.

Lark:

Ewww! Nasty.

Lucy:

I don't know.

He's pretty cute.

Lark:

Catch the bus then.

Lucy:

On my way.

Ten minutes later, both Lucy and Reid show up at my house. Lucy's wearing her multicolored sheep coat, and her hair is bright green.

"Coffee?" I offer.

Both shake their heads.

Lucy says, "That stuff is tar. I've had a kale smoothie today." She dances her head atop her shoulders. "My body is a temple, remember."

"Right. And your hair," I say, "hasn't got a single chemical in it."

"Whereas yours," she says, pointing at my fading red, "is needing some chemicals now." She fluffs a few bright-green strands. "Iona came over and persuaded me it was a good idea."

"It looks, um, good."

Outside, Reid gets in the car, and I join him in the front. Lucy stands outside the car and answers her cell while finishing a clove cigarette.

Before she gets in, Reid turns to me. "Larkette, have you had any other … *you* know?"

"You're doing that thing again. Where you don't make any sense at all. What are you talking about?" But I feel myself unpeeling.

He lets out a big sigh. "You know, what you told me happened to you at Fields Studios? I know you styled it out in front of Mr. Fields, but you were completely white-faced … I just wondered if it happened again."

"All fine here. No more seeing a hospital room and water seeping in —" My voice breaks. "But the messages — I keep thinking about them."

Lucy slumps in the back in a cloud of clove-cigarette aroma

and picks up the tail end of what I've said. "I've been thinking about déjà vu and what you told me. *Déjà vu* isn't quite right. Have you thought about *parallel* lives? They happen all the time!"

"No, they don't," Reid says.

"Anyway, I'm probably talking more about 'infinity points,'" Lucy says. "A parallel life is one that happens at the same time as the life you're currently living. Life as it could have been. Right? And, 'infinity point' is a scientific term. An infinity point is the place where parallel lines meet."

Reid lets out a small grunt of frustration. "Parallel lines don't meet."

Lucy tuts and keeps speaking. "Let's say the infinity point is at the lake. You had to make one of two choices, right? So you split in two."

"Guys, guys, this is all crazy. I'm just stressed after what happened at the lake and trying to focus on our show."

Reid stops the car for a red light.

"I think the lake is key — I think that's where it all goes back to. The number two means duality," Lucy says. "It represents your soul number. Your divinity." She checks her cell and reads: "'If you're open to receiving the message, angels will guide you.'"

"Where do you get this from?" I'm struggling to keep the incredulity out of my voice.

"All numbers are mystical," Lucy replies. "You're split into two lives. Two means something. It's a divine thing."

Reid parks his car. "You're saying that Lark is looking for angels."

"Stop it, guys."

"I'm worried." Reid leans back in his seat. "Lucy, I don't think this is helpful."

"If you want to go between the lives — I mean, to talk to your split self — I think you need to figure out the portal. That's all," she says.

"Portal to what?" My brain is hurting. Much as I hate to admit it, there is something about what she is saying that makes sense — much more sense than any of the other rationalizations I've had about the messages and the hallucinations. What if all of it is real?

"To the other life." She opens the car door but stays in her seat.

"Okay, just for the sake of argument or whatever, let's say you're right — but I don't want to be living some other life. I want to live this one. Even if I figured out the portal, why would I want to go to the other life? I could just *ignore* the messages."

"And the hallucinations? Didn't you say the one at Fields Studios was stronger than the one before?" Reid glances in the rearview mirror. He's about to say something else, it seems, but Lucy interrupts.

"What if they're getting more powerful? Why would that be?" Lucy asks.

I rub my forehead. "Maybe the other life is pulling me in. Maybe I don't actually want to live this life. I mean, no offense, guys, but I'm not having a lot of fun right now." I am only half joking.

"Perhaps Alec is the portal? You could go see him. Like research," Lucy says. She pauses, seeming to search for the right words. "Alec's parents are ... turning off his support machines, right? In how many days?"

"Seven." I close my eyes for a moment. I can't believe he's going to die. I can picture his eyes when we were in the canoe, full of light and life, and now this. My stomach lurches.

"In seven days he dies. That's a bad thing," Lucy says.

"Of course it's a bad thing!" I yell, choking up again.

"No, I mean, for your parallel lives. That'll be the end of it — I don't think one can end without it impacting the other one, if he's the portal ..."

"Why not?"

"This is insane, guys." Reid stares ahead out of the front window.

I'm busy checking my phone for visiting hours. "Well, that solves that," I say. I read out the notice displayed on the hospital website.

VISITORS RESTRICTED

After a surge in respiratory illnesses, the health region
is restricting visitors to the Pediatric and Pediatric
Intensive Care Wards to PARENTS ONLY.

"He's in Pediatrics?" Lucy asks.

"Until his birthday," I reply. "He's got his own room there. Remember, we saw his mom, when my dad was in the hospital."

She shrugs. "The universe will figure it all out. We should just go to school and get on with the day."

Reid frowns. "Larkette — I'm actually worried about you ..."

"This whole conversation is probably going to go down in our collective history as one of our wackiest," I say, trying to lighten the mood.

"I'm glad you're here with me now." Lucy gets out of the car and hip-checks me. "I mean, in this life."

Reid comes up alongside me. "I am, too," he says. "But this

parallel lives stuff isn't the right answer. I mean, perhaps you need to talk to someone or …"

His voice is thick with an emotion I can't place, but when I look at him, he's frowning again and checking his cell, acting like he's finished whatever it was he was going to say. I'm not sure I want to hear it, anyway. There's nothing to do but head in to school, as if a boy I went out with isn't about to die.

Day 41: too early

There is a painting on the wall. Where am I? Thick paint. A sunset. Or a sunrise. No, it's not a wall. It's a window: the window in my bedroom, the room in the house where I've always lived.

The sun sets and rises, sets and rises.

I try to draw breath. I'm lying in my bed, but I feel like I'm dropping, like in one of those terrifying dreams of falling. The sunrise and sunset move more and more quickly.

Someone else is in the room with me.

It's *me*. Moving quickly, like a flitting shadow. Moving *backward* around the room, out the room I go, in again, to the window, then away, to the desk. I watch, pinned to the bed, as my shadow-self flickers through the motions of her life in reverse. Growing younger, years racing by.

There I am taking the Tak, my guitar, from the wall — but because I'm watching everything in reverse, this was the day I put the Tak up there.

I see my mom. She's standing in the doorway to my room. There she is. I remember now — and I cannot believe I had forgotten. She watched me put my guitar up there, even though she could barely stand. She came to me.

I was so angry that day I couldn't speak to her.

Suddenly the scene stops reversing. Everything becomes real in time, with me lying on the bed watching.

"Lark," she says.

The fourteen-year-old version of me doesn't look at her, doesn't reply.

I struggle to sit up. I want to yell at my fourteen-year-old self to talk to Mom. To stop being so angry about missing the

191

stupid concert. To hold on to the Tak and play a song with it. With Mom. I want to shout at myself, *You only have twenty-one days left with her!*

Mom's face, because she was already exhausted from the effort of coming to my room, is pinched. She seems about to say something to younger me. But she doesn't speak either. We are in the same room, but we're a million light-years away from each other. I remember how much I hated her that day. How unfair is that, to hate someone for being sick?

The current version of me struggles again in the bed. I so badly need to sit up and tell them both —

And that's when it happens. Mom looks over at me. At the me who is here, watching the past.

She looks at me.

I smile at her.

And she smiles back.

I see then that I can't undo my anger with her when I was fourteen, but I also see that she doesn't mind. She forgives me. She'd already forgiven me.

I want to speak to her. I try to move my mouth, to ask all the questions I have — about the song she wrote for me but also about everything else. *Everything.*

She keeps smiling at me. A small, beautiful smile.

I stop trying to speak.

Stop.

I wake up gasping for breath.

I dress in my pastel jeans with the hole and a black T-shirt with a low back. I sling on a lacy sweater and spend a little time putting on mascara and giving myself smoky eyes.

Nifty:

Cole's bringing a bunch of friends to the show!

Lark:

Sweet.

Nifty:

Just wanted to say thanks —

things are going great.

Lark:

Am happy for you.

See you later. X

Nifty:

You okay? Been thinking about poor Alec.

They turn off the life support

in four days, right?

Lark:

I just want to go and see him.

To say goodbye.

The morning goes by in a blur — as if I'm still deep into the dream. I take my longboard and go down to the river for a while. I song-write until my head hurts. It's raining lightly, night is falling, and the cool damp air curls under my clothes.

I tug my fading hair into a short ponytail — it barely reaches, loose strands catching on my earrings. As I look up, the sky fills with raindrops — raindrops the size of soccer balls. They burst as they hit the sidewalk, and water spills from them, filling the street, rising up my legs.

It's happening again. A flicker at the edges, and I turn, aware of something pressing, something electric. There, almost like a hologram, yet infinitely more real, more human, is a figure. Oh, God, I *swear* I see myself standing in front of me.

It's *me*. I'm wearing the same jeans, the same shirt, the same everything. Even the same makeup, but my hair is long and black.

I'm there, and she — the other me — is talking to me. "Can you hear me?" she asks.

"Oh, my God. I can hear you," I reply.

But with another flicker, the other me is gone. And the sky clears, the rain stops, and nothing is changed. Yet everything is different.

Chapter Seven
Chapter Seven

Day 43: 3:53 p.m.

Quietly I sit by the river, drinking coffee, watching Alec balance on the beams underneath the bridge. He does an awesome flip from one and lands on both feet. I clap.

He comes over and flops next to me. "You're so pretty."

I blush.

"I guess you hear that all the time." He pushes me down gently, and we kiss.

The dampness of the ground seeps through my jacket. Alec slides a hand up my skirt and beneath my underwear. I moan as he touches me.

"I love you, Lark," he whispers, as he kisses the side of my neck.

There's a direct connection between my skin there and the rest of my body, which arches into him.

"I love you, too," I murmur.

He pulls back. "Say it again."

"Mmm. I love you. Don't stop."

He leans closer and kisses me all along the edge of my neck and down toward my bra line. Then he stops. Again. I groan.

He says, "Wanna go someplace more private?"

I glance around and pull myself to sitting. "Might be a good idea."

"My parents are home."

"My dad, too." I lean into him.

"This is impossible." He checks his cell. "I've got to be at work in thirty minutes."

I pull a face in frustration.

He jumps to his feet. "I'm going to get in a few more flips to distract me from how much I want to take all your clothes off."

He runs back toward the bridge and does a powerful jump. His hands grip a bar, and he swings himself up. My whole body tingles as I watch him.

A message comes in:

… two days Alec's family
is going to turn off the machines.
He'll die.

As if to emphasize how alive he is, Alec does a backflip from a low wall to land solidly on two feet. He grins at me.

In *her* life. He's going to die in her life.

But then what happens? Alec cannot die in her life. Because what then happens to him in mine? He balances with his arms out to steady himself as he walks along the low wall again.

The tiny stitches that hold me together are unpicked. I feel the threads coming loose. If there are only two days, I'm running out of time to figure out what to do next.

Alec does more flips, and I slump, looking at my phone, at a photo I took of my mom's lyrics:

You have to go
Back to the beginning
Jump
End it
To break
And resolve.

Back to the beginning? How do I get there? Maybe the other Lark has some idea — she spoke to me last time, although only for a moment. I wasn't strong enough to hold on to the connection between us — I wasn't strong enough to stay in her world.

But I could try again. Maybe she has answers. Maybe she can help me figure this out — it's not like I have anyone else to talk to about this. So I have to go to the portal — to Annabelle. I check the hospital update and discover that the restrictions on visiting Pediatrics have just been lifted. Finally, finally, visitors are allowed. I look up visiting times — and see that I could go now. Alec does a last flip and comes over to me.

"I'm going to work. You want to come over after?" he asks, breathing heavily.

"Sure."

Alec doesn't seem to notice that I'm distracted, and before he goes, he kisses me and murmurs again that he loves me.

Part of me falls into the kiss, the feel of him, the warmth

of him. Another part of me is thinking about getting to the hospital. Finding Annabelle. Going to the other Lark and telling her we have to keep Alec alive.

I arrive at the hospital and press the button for the elevator. I tap my fingers on my leg impatiently, and after watching the lights change on the third then fourth floors, I give up waiting and decide to take the stairs. When I get to Annabelle's room, the door is shut. I nudge it open.

The first thing I notice is that Suzanne is there. I step back quickly and wander away from the door. I'll just have to wait. Ten minutes go by, twenty. About half an hour after I arrive, Suzanne steps out of the room and goes over to talk to the nurses. Then she gets out her cell phone and takes off down the hallway to make a call. I glance at the nurse on Reception, who's looking the other way. There's nothing wrong with what I'm doing, I reassure myself, not entirely believing it. Three nurses are deep in conversation over at a desk. None of them notices me. No one stops me as I slip into Annabelle's room.

Her freshly brushed hair is spread out over the pillow. If she weren't in a coma, she'd look like she was sleeping, but the beeps of the machines and the stillness in her face remind me otherwise. The room smells of fresh flowers; the dead ones have finally been replaced. I sit next to Annabelle. I wouldn't be doing this if I didn't have to. I think about Alec. About how I want to live a life with him. How he cannot die, not in any life. She'll understand. The other Lark will understand. Together we'll make this work.

I take Annabelle's hand. A terrible groan comes from the

ceiling, and I shiver, holding on tightly to Annabelle's hand as I look up. As I watch, cracks form, and the plaster darkens with the stain of water. The ceiling bulges and then splits as if it's a huge, pale egg, and water cascades.

I am washed away.

Day 43: 3:53 p.m.

I flip my short hair into a low pony, pick up my longboard and wander into the corner store with an urge for chocolate. Since I saw myself two days ago, I've been sick to my stomach, wondering what she was trying to say. All I heard was "Can you hear me?" But then she was gone.

A shudder passes through my body, and something worse than nausea. I'm reminded of something I'd long forgotten. I threw up on the day Mom told me she was going to die. *There's nothing more they can do.* I bent over the toilet bowl, and she held back my hair. Right now I'm just as nauseated. The damp makes me feel like I'm sweating.

I select a chocolate bar and then, checking that the clerk isn't looking, slide it into my pocket. The thrill is immediate. Everything clears from my head. I take a deep breath and relish the feeling. Stealing is even more powerful than songwriting in the way it makes me feel in control, calm, cool.

I glance over my shoulder. The clerk is serving someone else. Without buying anything, the stolen chocolate bar in my pocket, I hurry toward the door —

The hand on my shoulder isn't a shock. It's as if I've been waiting for this to happen. *This is it.* A security guard has caught me, and when I turn around, my life will be in his hands. It's a relief, actually, to have someone else make a decision.

But it's not a security guard. It's *Iona.* She's wearing skinny black jeans, a chain-mail tank, a light jacket — and a furious expression. She tugs me toward her and hugs me. Except her grip is forceful as she drags me back inside the store.

"What the hell are you doing, Lark?" she growls in my ear.

At the same time, she takes the chocolate bar from my pocket. "You bonehead."

I push her off. "What's it to you?"

"Come on, we're getting out of here." She chucks the chocolate bar on the counter and pays for it. The clerk is glaring at both of us. Iona drags me out of the store and down an alleyway. She lets me go and says, "Come with me."

I'm shivering as she leads me down toward the river, and I'm surprised she's not freezing in what she's wearing.

"Iona, I'm going to be late to meet Reid."

She doesn't look at me. "Tell him you were kidnapped. Whatever."

"Fine." I lean my longboard against a bench, hoping no one will steal it, before we make our way down a narrow, steep path, through the trees, to a small clearing that overlooks the water.

"So," she says, throwing the chocolate bar at me, "you need to tell me what's going on."

"Since when are you the police?"

She laughs. "Nice try, tough girl. What is *with* you? You can't just steal shit."

"Stop it."

"You're actually a good girl. With a good future. Unless you screw it up with a criminal record."

"It's a chocolate bar."

"You really are an idiot. They don't care how big the object is. It's theft." She squats and pulls out a packet of cigarettes. "I *have* a conviction for theft, Lark." She lights a cigarette and passes it to me. When I try to wave it away, she says, "Yes, I know you don't smoke, but … just …"

I take the cigarette and squat next to her. I put it in my mouth, and she lights it. I've never really liked smoking, but as I inhale this time, I feel a heady sensation that momentarily distracts me. I cough a little and take another drag.

"Superdumb," she says. "I stole a pair of jeans. I don't want to talk about it. But it is a big deal. Just so you know."

I look at her and wonder when this all happened. I see her every day at school. Twice a week at band practice. I've known her since we were babies. I think about the secrets we all keep, the layers to all our lives and the way we never really know anyone. The way we never really know ourselves. We smoke together for a few quiet minutes.

"I'm living a parallel life. I really am."

Iona flicks ash from her cigarette but stays silent.

I continue, unable to stop now. "I saw my parallel self. I keep getting messages, stuff that shows me glimpses of my other life. And my mom believed this, too — I'm not crazy, Iona. So I wonder if I could go back to that moment — what if I was quicker? — you know, at the lake. What if I didn't take so long to decide what to do?"

"You can't go back, Lark. You of all people should know that." Iona lights another cigarette with the one she's finishing.

"You're talking about my mom?"

"Aren't you?"

I look out over the river. "Maybe," I confess. "Maybe I am."

She stands. "I have no idea what's happening to you, Lark. You're writing the best songs ever, and you've been rocking it at band, but this other stuff makes it sound like you're out of your tree." She inhales deeply. "I don't mean to be harsh. But this is what I'm going to do." She exhales a smoke ring. "You're going to freaking lose it, but I'm calling your dad."

"What?"

"You won't stop. The stealing — it's a thing. Like, I'm not going to get all therapy on you, but you're going to tell me you've stopped. You'll think you have stopped. But you won't. And then … well, that's just what I'm going to do."

"You are *not* calling my dad. I'm not a little kid."

"Lark, seriously, you think you're living in a parallel world. You need help."

"I AM LIVING PARALLEL LIVES!"

Her eyes widen, and for a moment she looks genuinely scared. She takes a step back. "Take it easy."

"Iona, don't do this. I can handle it."

She turns and walks away from me.

"Iona, what the hell!"

But she's gone.

Five minutes later, Dad calls. I don't answer. I don't know what to say to him. He calls again. Then messages:

Dad:

Answer your phone.

Dad:

You seriously

need to answer.

Pick up now.

Dad:

Lark. NOW.

I put my phone in my pocket and board to D'Lish. Reid stands outside.

"Sorry I'm late," I say, about to give him a hug.

"Iona messaged me." He holds up his phone.

"What is she *doing*? I'm already dealing with my dad."

I push open the door to the café, trying to keep things light. But he doesn't follow me in. We're left standing by the open door.

"Lark, she says you've been stealing stuff. She said you were acting crazy —"

"It's not her place to tell you. Or Dad. Jesus. This is all happening too fast."

"What do you expect her to do?"

"I told her about the parallel lives. That's all."

"The parallel-life stuff? Larkette, that's just Lucy. The thing is —" He runs his hands through his hair. "Well, I understand why it's interesting. I mean the psychology of it. Alternate lives. You know, for my family, I mean. If we'd never left Iraq, what would my life be like now? Who would I be?"

"See, you get it."

"No, that's not what I'm saying."

"Think about it. It's the sort of question that opens, right? We don't know if my mom is somewhere, in some other life, or if your family were killed in the Iraq War; we don't know if Alec is fine in another life; we don't know any of it. But I don't want to spend the rest of my life bumping into what my life could have been, being pulled out of one existence to another and back again."

"See, when you start talking about your mom like that ..." He grimaces. "Larkette ... Lucy's a flake. We all love her. But she's a flake. There's no such thing as parallel lives."

"What do you know?" My voice is louder than I intend. Inside, customers look up from their tables. Lucy, who is behind the counter, pulls a face. I yank the door shut.

"The shoplifting — Iona says it's a big deal. It *is* a big deal."

"It was a chocolate bar. Or whatever." I stare at the wind blowing through the branches of the trees. Anywhere rather than at Reid.

"That's what she said you'd say. She's putting herself out there — telling us about it."

"Tattling on me! Like we're little kids!"

"I mean she told me about *her*. How bad it was. And she thinks that's what you're doing. She also said that the parallel-life stuff is a coping mechanism."

I hit the wall in frustration. "In two days, Alec's family is going to turn off the machines. He'll die. Which is terrible in itself. But which life do I end up in if that's the case? Which one do I want?" Trying to answer my own questions makes me feel dizzy. I hear Suzanne again: *Lark! DO SOMETHING!* I rub my temples.

"Lark, I think you … maybe you need help. I looked into how to get a meeting with the school counselor — it's pretty easy."

"You know what? I thought you were on my side. Even though you obviously don't believe me, I thought you *cared*. But forget it. Just stay away from me, Reid."

"Don't do this. Don't get angry with me."

I narrow my eyes. "You and Iona can make up your stupid stories about me — but you know what? I'm not doing this."

"Doing what?"

"I'm not taking part in this — you guys and your intervention or whatever it is you think you're doing. And screw the show." I put one earbud in. I turn Neko Case on superloud.

"Larkette, calm down. You're living for the show right now."

"No. I'm not. I'm *out*." My whole heart cries, *No! Not the show!* But I'm too angry to stop myself. "Tell the others whatever you like. Tell them I'm completely crazy. But there's no way I'm putting up with this crap."

"Don't do this."

"It's already done." I put in the other earbud and board to the river. When I get there, I flip my board up and slump against a tree, staring at the water. Even over the music, I can hear Suzanne's desperate cry.

Lucy:
Lovers' tiff?

Lark:
Reid is NOT my lover.

Lucy:
Touchy.
See you later?

I don't answer. There's a whooshing sound in my ears, like I'm listening to a conch shell and the ocean is roaring toward me. What if Reid and Iona are right? What if I am crazy? And how could I give up the show? But there's no way I'm sticking with the band if they won't stick with me. I try to take a breath. The sky cracks open; drops of rain fall, quickly becoming a deluge. *No. No! NO!*

Day 43

My body is being crushed by water. This is so much worse than last time. My long hair tangles and gets everywhere. I struggle to calm down, to swim, to find myself. I pull myself upward, seeking the surface. I cannot hold my breath any longer — I am going to die.

I break through and gulp huge mouthfuls of the sweet air. I am here. At least, I am not where I was. I have survived.

In this life, I'm by the river.

We're by the river.

Lark sits with her knees up, her back resting against a tree. Her face is pale, her expression bleak. Her bobbed red hair is in a low pony. She takes out her earbuds, her eyes filling with terror.

The same terror rises in me like a wave crashing against the shore. I press the back of my hand to my mouth. I'm going to vomit. She is there. She is me.

She seems to recover before I do. Her face regaining color. Her expression changing from fear to determination. I'm bigger than I thought I was somehow, and my cheekbones are more defined than I've ever realized. I'm both a stranger and not.

I say, "Can you hear me?"

She nods.

A rush of the same determination I see in her fills me. I am here for a reason. And I do not know how much time I have. The words rush from me: "Alec and I are in love. We have to save him. In both our lives. I can't bear it. What if him dying in your life kills him in my life? You know he's about to die in your life, right? Two days. I got the message from —"

"You're right. Alec's parents have decided to …" She doesn't finish her sentence.

"So the messages I get seem to be a bleed-through — stuff from your life seeping into mine? Like the wrong radio frequency bleeding through into the channel you're trying to listen to."

"That makes a weird sort of sense."

"Nothing makes sense. Okay, so …" I try to stay focused, try to think what to do. I haven't planned this, and I don't even know what to ask. "How about we go back to the beginning. That's what Mom's song says to do."

"Mom's song? I don't know what you mean."

"You didn't get the letter?"

"No — Dad was so sick …"

"What do you mean? Is he okay?"

"I think so."

"Oh, God, I … we have to stay in this life. In this life, Dad is fine. He's not seriously sick. The beginning. We have to go back. Think: What exactly did you do that day? I mean, at the lake. That's when all this started, right?"

"Nothing. I mean, at first, I didn't know what to do. I froze."

"So did I."

"Suzanne was pleading. Telling me to do something."

"Yes. Same here. But I didn't know what to do." I remember the time passing.

"It didn't seem very long." She runs her hands through her short hair. "But by then it was too late to save them both."

"Do you think we could have? Saved them both, I mean?"

"We'll never know. Once I finally got moving, I turned to Annabelle."

"How could you leave Alec? There was no one near him. I was the only one. He was already under." I remember how I pushed myself under his heavy arms, treading water madly, holding him up. He was losing consciousness, his eyes closing. *She's not breathing!* Martin's voice carried over the water. Alec leaned his wet head against me. I kicked and floundered —

"How could you pick Alec over Annabelle?" she asks, interrupting the memory. "How could you pick him over her?"

I fold my arms across my chest.

"She's a child. I swam as fast as I could toward her. When I reached her, I was coughing and spitting lake water, but I grabbed her. It was hard to get my arms around her red life jacket, but I managed to turn her face up. Her skin was the color of dusk. Then she coughed up a plume of water, gagging and spluttering."

"There was no one near Alec. You should have saved him."

"Yeah? Well, I didn't. What do you want? How did you even get here?"

"By going to Annabelle — she's like a doorway, a portal to you."

"Lucy talked about portals."

"Right, okay, but the point is I'm here to tell you that we have to save him now. From them turning off his machines. Because I'm not sure how this all works, Lark. But what if him dying in your life means he dies in mine? I can't bear it. You don't get it: he's the love of our lives. You have to stop them pulling the plug. Tell them he's alive."

"He's alive in your life, but he's in a coma in mine. Think about it — you want me to go to the hospital and tell them to keep him alive, against the advice of the doctors, because he's alive in a parallel world?" She stands.

"Do you have any other ideas?"

"Why do you even think it's going to affect your life with him? I mean … maybe everything will be fine." But she doesn't look convinced.

"Maybe. I'm just scared, Lark. I can't live without him. I can't."

"You're asking me to go to the hospital and talk about parallel lives with a family that is losing their son. I can't say something like that. Anyway, they'll think I'm crazy. I've had enough of everyone thinking I'm making all this up — like Reid."

"Reid? I've hardly spoken to him in weeks. What else is going on in your life?"

"They all think I'm crazy for shoplifting … that's why I quit the show. Even though Martin Fields will be there."

"Shoplifting?" She glares at me but doesn't speak. "Okay. Whatever."

I hold up my hands.

"The show?" I say. "Martin Fields is going? Wow."

"Yeah. But not me. Like I said, everyone thinks I'm losing my mind. So they can just go ahead without me."

"I'm not doing the show either. I haven't been to practices — I'm not ready. I've been spending all my time with Alec."

"Alec, Alec, Alec. Will you listen to yourself?" she murmurs. "Who even are you?"

"Who the hell are you?" I spit, suddenly angry at her judging me.

We fall silent, staring at each other.

A whoosh of water floods over me.

"Wait!" I say. "We still have to figure this out. We've got to stop fighting each other. We're in this together —"

Then I'm swept up by frigid water, and I struggle to keep from drowning. This time it's even more terrifying. I cannot survive this — I'm going to die. But moments later, I'm back in the hospital room, where the doctor with oddly colored eyes is angrily telling me to let go of Annabelle's hand.

Chapter Eight

Chapter Eight

Day 44: late morning

Dad is out. I'm skipping school. Alec and I are in my bed, and he has pinned my arms above my head, our hands entwined in my long hair, the covers half over our almost-naked bodies. He stares into my eyes.

We're listening to Glass Animals. My favorite of their songs is coming to an end. The possibility of this ending tomorrow is killing me. Alec, who is supposed to have his birthday tomorrow. Alec, who is kissing me now, softly at the corner of my mouth. But I don't know what else to do — unless I try to get to Annabelle again. But I'm pretty sure the hospital has Annabelle's room on lockdown after yesterday — the doctor was furious at me for breaking into Pediatrics. I can only hope that Lark in the other life is going to do something. I feel paralyzed. That's what it is — just like I felt on the lake that day. And then I don't. Instead I feel his hands on my skin, his breath in my ear, his body pushing against mine. I want this. Oh, I want this now.

Alec slides my underwear down. It tangles momentarily at my ankles, but then I kick it from my feet. He runs his hand up my inner thigh. His stubble rubs against my cheek. I still have my hands in my hair, and when I try to bring them down to touch him, he uses one hand to grip them above my head, like he did once before. He teases me with kisses on each corner of my mouth, then trails kisses down my neck to my collarbone. I arch my body toward him, my breasts and stomach against his hard chest and abs. He opens my legs with his and pushes me into the bed. I gasp and close my eyes. The music washes over me, lyrics about sleeping with someone else. I wonder what the other me is doing — is she sleeping with someone else?

Alec says, "Are you crying?"

"I'm fine."

"Just fine?"

"More than fine. Don't stop."

Later, we get dressed and hit the kitchen before Dad comes home — he left early this morning without realizing that Alec had spent the night. Alec heads to the washroom, and I message Nifty:

Lark:
Hope tonight goes well.

Nifty:
Thanks for nothing.

Lark:

Nifty, don't be like that.

Then I text Reid:

Lark:

Get Nifty to forgive me.

Have such a great night.

Reid:

We'll miss you.

Lark:

Next time — promise.

We'll work this out.

Alec comes up behind me, and I jump, sliding the phone, facedown, across the table.

"You're messaging Reid?" he asks.

"Is that a big deal?"

He shakes his head, but not before I've seen his jaw clench. "'Course not."

"I was just wishing the band luck tonight."

He sits down across from me. I reach over the table to hold his hand. The house smells of the coffee we're brewing. I say, "Should we use travel cups? Go for a walk?"

He flips over my hand and traces a pattern on my palm. When the coffee is ready, I watch him fill our mugs. I need to be in the moment and not anticipating the future, not stressing about what will happen to Alec if he dies in the other life. I need to be with him right now. If being split into parallel lives has taught me anything, it's to live the one life I've got the best I can.

We walk and walk, drinking our coffees. When we get hungry, we decide to stop to grab take-out sandwiches. The decision isn't one we really talk about; we're just hungry, and so we eat. Mom told me once that what she loved about my dad was that the relationship was easy. With Alec it's easy. Time vanishes; the hours slip by.

We hold hands, loosely, comfortably, and neither of us speaks for a while. I wonder how the band is doing, and my feet lead us toward Lydia's.

Grinning goofily, we swing hands as we walk. I can't help but peek through the window of Lydia's, even though if Nifty or anyone else spotted me, it would be the worst. The band's onstage. And Nifty is singing in my place.

"He's good." Alec's voice makes it clear he's impressed.

"Yeah, I guess."

We turn to the river. Once we've found a secret, sandy patch, we start gathering sticks to build a little fire. We listen to music on my earbuds together, Alec huddled to my right. It's all very primitive and modern. Night falls. We talk about nothing and everything. I watch the flames and feel the heat on my hands, the chill at my back. A memory of hearing Alec's dad shout through their front door echoes inside me. I think about how Alec mentioned problems at home. Pieces sift and fall like icing sugar, and a pattern appears.

"Alec, can I ask you something?"

"Sure." He puts his hands behind his head and leans back on the grass.

"You know that time you had a bruise. Was it ... was it your dad who did that?"

Alec looks straight up at the sky. "Do you know the name of that star?"

I rest my head against his chest. I follow his lead and lightly tease him. "You're pulling the star-gazing trick?"

"Yeah," he says, sliding one arm under my waist. "I tell you the name of stars, then get into your pants. Oh, I forgot, I already got into your pants."

I giggle and kiss him on his chin. We fall quiet.

"My dad hits me, yeah. Not all the time. He's great, really. But then he gets mad. It's like a flipped switch. So yes, the bruise was from him. It's why I was stressed out for a while."

"Sorry. I don't mean to ..."

"S'okay. He won't let us leave. Says it looks bad. Mom gets the worst of it, but when I'm around, I try to keep him off her. Sometimes I win. Sometimes he does." He clicks his tongue against his bottom lip, the piercing there momentarily catching the firelight.

"Can't you call the police?"

He clenches his jaw. Shadows flicker across his face. "I don't want him to end up in jail. Even thinking about it makes me ..."

He doesn't finish the sentence. He sits up, shifts me from his chest and kisses me on the top of my head.

We kiss for a while. But I can tell he's distracted, and the conversation about his dad has made him sad.

"Wanna do some climbing?" I ask. "The bridge is right here."

Alec nods. He douses the fire with a can of pop.

Reid:

Feeling okay?

Second set doesn't start for 30 mins —

if you're even feeling a bit better, come …

Alec sees it. His face clouds. "Booty call?"

"No, Alec. Of course not."

He nods minimally, refusing to look at me.

"Come on, let's climb."

He scrambles up the slope, and I follow.

"Alec, wait. He's just a friend."

He calls back, "It's no big deal."

The words say one thing, but his tone says the opposite.

"You know I love you, right?" I say.

He pulls himself onto the bridge. I try to catch up, but he's already hitched himself onto the metal slats above me and is moving like a monkey. I scramble and heave myself, my muscles tight, my breath heavy, the fresh breeze doing nothing to cool me down.

I look down. The water below is inky. The current is hard to detect from this height, but somehow I have a sense of the river flowing, and I imagine myself being pulled along. I start to tremble, and my muscles tighten more, making it impossible to climb.

"Alec, don't be like this," I call up to him.

"Then stop lying to me about Reid."

I slow my breathing and make myself focus. I move one hand, then one foot — slowly, slowly, concentrating. I come abreast of Alec as he's sitting on one of the large horizontal metal beams. It's maybe a third of a yard wide and about the length of a swimming pool, connecting two diagonal metal struts. It's rusted. I rub a finger over it, find it cold and rough. Tears prick at my eyes, and my cheeks feel flushed. I smile at him, hoping he'll get out of this mood.

"I'm not lying about Reid, Alec." I slide closer to him.

He says very softly, "But you are lying, Larkette. Don't think I haven't heard him call you that."

"He's my friend."

"You think you can play games with me." He grabs my arm, and his grip is hard. Hard enough to bruise me. Fingers of shock seize at my heart.

"Alec, please." He doesn't let go; if anything, he tightens his hold. "Alec, you're hurting me."

"Yeah. That's what happens when you hurt me." His eyes glitter. "I trusted you with … with all that stuff about my dad."

"You hardly told me anything!"

"Just as well, when you do this."

"Do what? Get a text message?"

"From your boyfriend."

"Let me go."

"Not until you tell me the truth."

"You're not yourself."

"You're the one who's leading Reid on. Do you know what I did to my last girlfriend? She thought it was okay to sleep around, too."

"To Sharbat? What did you do?"

He tightens his vicelike hold. "What the hell do you think happens to liars?"

His angry shout sounds exactly like his dad's.

"This isn't you, Alec." But as I say it, I see things I've been ignoring. How he pushed me harder than I wanted for us to take the next step physically. But I wanted to. At least, I did in the end. Earlier, he was always assertive. That's all this is. He's asserting himself. He'd never hurt me. Except he is hurting me. My arm …

I try to shake him off. I've been passive, but now I'm fighting. The beam is too narrow for any sort of struggle. We both wobble precariously.

"Alec! Careful. We're too high. We could fall."

His grip comes loose, and I yank my arm toward myself. Like the train has passed along the tracks, Alec's anger is gone. I see in his eyes my Alec. Suddenly he's afraid, too.

I pull away from him. "I'm leaving, Alec."

"Don't go." His expression is filled with remorse.

"There's somewhere I've got to be."

He reaches for me, but I'm already backing away along the beam, then turning, starting the climb down, away, away, away. If he followed, he'd be faster, and the fear of this spurs me on. But he doesn't follow. He stays, a silent shadow far above.

Day 44: dawn

I make coffee and wrap up in a coat to go and sit outside as the dawn rises. I can't believe that I ended up arguing with myself when she came to me — and what if she's right? What if Alec is the love of our lives? Regardless. His parents can't end his life when he's alive in another world. Can they?

Dad surprises me when he puts his hand on my shoulder. He, too, is holding a coffee cup. His face is stern.

"Never do that again. Never ignore my calls."

His voice is very low and quiet — which only happens when he's deadly serious. He steps down so he's in front of me, and then he squats and stares me full in the face.

"Dad ... can we talk about this later?"

"Are you kidding?" he explodes. "You don't answer your phone. You come home while I'm out looking for you, worried sick. You pretend to be asleep when I come into your room."

"I wasn't pretending. I was tired."

"You know what, Lark? You don't get to ignore your phone like that. You don't get to steal. You don't get to behave like this."

"I know that."

"You're not acting like you *know* anything. Iona was very brave to call me. Not a lot of seventeen-year-olds have got that kind of sense. Certainly not my own daughter."

"Okay, okay, enough."

He puts his cup down hard on the ground. "No, it is not enough. Do you understand how much trouble you're in? Do you even remotely realize what you're throwing away if you get caught? Stealing a chocolate bar is the same in the eyes of a store as stealing money from the till. They come down on you like a ton of bricks. Your whole future — college, jobs, everything — you're risking it all. And what the hell is all this stuff about parallel lives?"

I catch a glimpse of fear in his eyes. "Of course you don't believe me either."

He lifts his hands to his hair. "It's too much."

"But it's actually happening. I'm living two lives."

"You need to stop this, Lark. We need help. This is out of control. You are forbidden to leave the house except for school."

"You're grounding me? There's no way I'm going to school."

"And you're going to a counselor as soon as we can make an appointment."

"You can't ground me."

"I'll allow the show — I won't make you miss that."

"I already quit, Dad. I'm not singing with those traitors."

"They are your friends. Iona is trying to help you."

"Some help." I stand and turn to go into the house. "I'd better start my prison sentence now."

"Lark, we are not done talking."

"We are so done talking," I yell, as I slam the door behind me and make my way upstairs.

In my room, I listen to music and think about Alec lying in a coma for the last full day of his life. I remember our day on the lake together. I remember how the other Lark talked about him. She came to my life on purpose, to talk to me, to figure out a way to make this separation in ourselves stop. And if she can get to me, then maybe *I can get to her*. What did Lucy say about portals? Could a portal take me to her the way she came to me?

Is there a portal in my life? What portal? She said Annabelle was hers. Is mine Alec? But his parents will soon turn off his life support.

I spend a couple of hours, my head pounding, trying to figure out a way to solve all this. I fall asleep — it's always been my way of dealing with stress. When my mom died, I slept like I would never wake. It's just the same as when I hesitated at the lake, not knowing what to do. I am paralyzed. And so I sleep. I try to wake, but I tumble into strange dreams and scary thoughts. Alec will die.

Dad knocks at my door. I mumble for him to leave me alone. So he does. I fall back asleep.

In my dream, I am back at the lake. With no time and a choice to make. I'm in the water between Alec and Annabelle. Suzanne is screaming at me. One second goes by, two seconds, three. But I cannot move. I cannot decide what to do. Four seconds, five, six.

Seven —

I sit bolt upright.

I yank on a sweater and slip down the stairs. Dad is on his phone in the kitchen, his back to me, talking softly, his voice not sounding like his own. He doesn't turn around, doesn't hear me as I leave. Night has already fallen. The day has gone.

But it's not too late. It can't be. There has to be a way to fix this. And I am done with doing *nothing*.

I longboard to the hospital. Outside Alec's room, a gathering of his family is quietly chatting, some weeping. I see his mom talking with a woman who looks like her — her sister, maybe?

Farther down the hallway, an older couple hold hands. They don't speak at all.

I wonder — what if I should have saved him instead? How could I put these people through this? What if he is the love of my life? But what about Annabelle? She's a little girl.

But maybe my other life is better. What have I got in this one? Everyone's angry with me for stealing. And I'm not even going to be in the show that I've dedicated my heart and soul to since the drowning.

Alec's mother looks up. She catches my eye. "Lark. Hello." She clicks toward me in her heels.

"Sorry. I just …"

"It's okay. I should have called you. I know you wanted to see him. To say goodbye —" Her voice catches.

"I … it's tomorrow, right?"

She nods.

In my mind, I hear Suzanne. *Lark! DO SOMETHING!*

But I can't. I can't urge Alec's mom not to turn off his life support. I can't talk about parallel lives.

So. I am still paralyzed after all.

"Come," she says. "Come and see him."

Alec lies slightly to one side of the bed. My footsteps make quiet taps as I pass the window to sit beside him. The room smells warm and musty. A monitor beeps, its thin wires connected to Alec's chest, which is half exposed by the turned-down sheet. The top three buttons on his pajamas are open.

"Please, not too long," Alec's mom says. "I'll be out here — I have to talk to my parents. We're all saying our goodbyes today."

I nod, my throat tight. What a choice she's making. I think of the other Lark begging me to ask for Alec to stay alive. I think about how our lives are so much made of the choices we make. How just a few seconds of indecision in the lake has impacted everything since then.

Alec's mom closes the door lightly. I touch the gray blanket. Alec's hair is clean, his face, too. His lip piercing and the fading mark on his temple are the only things marring his features — otherwise he'd look like a young boy.

"I'm sorry," I whisper. "I'm sorry I didn't ..." He can't hear me. That's why his mom is making this choice. He's already gone. This isn't the Alec I went to the lake with, not the one who pulled off his shirt and dived in to save a little girl. This is just a shell.

And maybe a portal. The word comes to me from the conversation I had with Lucy, and from the other Lark telling me that Annabelle was the portal in her life. But how? God, this is all crazy. I reach for Alec's hand to calm my jittery brain.

The windowpane shatters, and water gushes toward me, fills the room, filling me with terror. I'm choking. I am drowning, dying. I thrash and flail, an unthinking creature, fighting only to survive. But then I see a shimmering window. A window to another life. I swim toward it.

There she is. She is walking through the darkness, running now. Just as quickly as I was underwater, I'm through and breathing cool, fresh air. She keeps running. Frantically I call her name, but no sound comes out. This is too hard. I am being pulled back.

No. I won't let go. I won't until I catch her. I drag myself through the window, fighting the undertow. I feel like I'm tearing through a thin layer of cellophane, something, because suddenly I am standing on the dark street, the air cool around me.

I orient myself. We're three blocks from the river. Lark runs along a narrow alleyway, away from the river, toward a busier street.

"Lark," I yell. This time my voice works. But she's too far ahead to hear me.

Suddenly I understand. Home. She's going to our house. I catch my breath as I watch her run inside. I'm shaking with exertion — this is so hard.

Chapter Nine
Chapter Nine

Day 44: night

I run away from the bridge, away from Alec and the pain he caused me. I run through the city and back to my room. I think I hear someone call my name. I feel a shimmering, but I don't pause. I can't stop now.

I find the video that Mom left me, and even though I don't have much time, I know I need to watch it; it's short, only three minutes. I need her now; I need her more than ever. In it, she's close to the camera, and her expression is full of her love for me. I have watched it many times, but this time I see myself in her in a way I never have before — my face is like her face; my eyes are like her eyes.

"I'm always there," she finishes. "I love you, Lark."

Mom was wrong. She isn't always there. She's always here, in the choices I make, in the songs I write, in me.

I glance at my Tak where it hangs on the wall. She has given me the strength to do this.

I take it down.

With my guitar in my hands, I walk out of my room.

I follow the other Lark into our bedroom. She doesn't see me — I guess my connection isn't as powerful as the one she had. I watch her as she watches the video Mom left us. I watch her reach for our Tak.

"ALEC!" someone yells.

But suddenly there's water around my ankles, surging up, engulfing me.

I am washed back to the hospital room. Alec lies on the bed, and his eyes are fixed on me. "Alec," I scream. His eyes close.

No. No. No.

"Alec," I scream again.

Alec's mom runs into the room.

"He opened his eyes. He opened his eyes," I say.

"Oh, my baby boy," his mom cries. She calls for a nurse.

For a moment, I am shaking too much to move. Then I realize I'm running out of time. I have to go. I back out of the room.

"Lark, wait," Alec's mom says.

"I'm sorry," I reply. "I have to do this."

I have to stitch myself back together. I have to make myself whole. And I think I know how.

I race to my house to pick up my Tak. As I hold it, everything feels like it's starting to make sense. I hurry to Lydia's, where I find the rest of the band sitting together at a booth. I'm a shattered mirror, glass shards all over the place. My hands are trembling. My dad sits with them. A woman with long red hair perches next to him, holding his hand. No way. She's smiling at him in a doe-eyed, happy way.

Reid sees me and pushes through the people between us. He leans over me and says, "You made it."

I smile at him. "Hey," I say to everyone at the table. "Look, guys, I'm sorry. I'm sorry I've been stealing stuff. I will get help for that. But I need you to believe me. Believe that we don't know everything. Okay? Just for tonight?"

Iona rolls her eyes. But my dad surprises me. He takes my hand and says, "I believe you."

My throat tightens.

"Your mother would have been happy to hear me say that." Dad lets out a long sigh.

"Why didn't you?"

"I can't undo it now, Lark. And you know what? It doesn't matter now. It never did. If she got a choice or she didn't, if she had two lives … I still only have one. And I have to live it without her."

I hug him and straighten up. "So, can I play?"

Nifty gets up and kisses me on the cheek. "Yay! We all still love you, Lark. Onward, soldiers!"

"Since you've got your good guitar, you'd better get on and play," Dad says. He gestures at the woman next to him. "This is Alyssa, by the way."

I smile at her. "Nice to meet you."

Reid grabs my hand. Sparks run from his skin to mine, and I glance over at him. Maybe, maybe, he and I have a future. In one life. In some life.

"Come on," he says. "Time for us to go on."

Iona winks a panda-painted eye. "Rock chick, you'd better be good."

I walk into Lydia's, and my hands are trembling. The rest of the band are sitting together at a booth. And my dad is with them.

"Hey," I say. "Look, guys, I'm sorry. I'm sorry I've been so caught up with Alec. Please let me play the next set with you."

Iona winks a panda-painted eye. "Rock chick, you'd better be good."

Her words surround me like buzzing flies. I stumble onto the stage, and I don't know what to sing. Standing here is awkward and clunky. I'm awkward and clunky. I look at the others — they must regret having me on. But they meet my panicked stare with smiles and eyebrow raises. *Go, Lark, go,* they seem to be saying. *You can do this.*

We start with silence, letting the anticipation build. I close my eyes briefly and feel the music rise in me. I'm holding my Tak, and I send a message to my mother in my mind: *I hope you enjoy this.*

First I sing one of the songs I've been working on — "Colony" — and then I do the one about choices and freedom and being split in two:

"I'm shattered glass
Shatter me, me, me

A moment in pieces
Take a shard of me
Look deeply inside for remnants
Of how we used to be
Part the water, slide in a ripple
Find yourself in time
Find me."

As we progress from song to song, I fill myself with the feeling, let it rise through me.

I do it. I sing old songs until we have time for one more song. I don't know for certain where the impulse comes from — but suddenly I'm sure what I want to sing next. The words come to me as fluid as water. I turn to the band.

"Guys, will you do something with me?"

Iona nods, flashing me a smile. Nifty frowns, Reid, too.

I let my fingers play the opening notes. My Tak feels alive in my hands. Nifty — after a pause — gets into it and backs me up. Iona hits the drums. Reid joins us on the keyboard, a fast, repetitive melody.

Someone sings. Is it me?

"A second world, another life
I could have lived, I could have loved
Parallel you
Parallel me ..."

*

We're about to finish, when I turn to the band. "Guys, will you do something with me?"

Iona grins. Nifty frowns, and Reid, too.

But I know the right song to finish this.

I let my fingers play the opening notes. The Tak feels electric in my hands. Nifty gets into it and backs me up. Iona hits the drums. Reid joins us on the keyboard, a fast, repetitive melody.

Someone sings. Is it me?

"A second world, another life
I could have lived, I could have loved
Parallel you
Parallel me
No matter how I want it
Or wish it differently
I can only be me
Only me
Let go of the other life
No need to do this differently
Be me
Be free."

My mother. It's her voice. Her song is beautiful. But there's more to it than that. Suddenly the words of the song unravel — I am songwriting as I sing:

"A second world, another life
I could have lived, I could have loved
Parallel you
Parallel me."

The band takes up the whole room with sound, the words vibrate from my mouth, and the crowd moves a little, then more.

"This is the song
That tells my story
I am only me
I am free
Let go of the other life
No need to do this differently
Be me
Be free."

I realize that I am free now — free of the paralysis that has held me since that moment in the lake. Cracks appear along the walls. Water trickles and then pours. I don't stop singing:

"I am free
I am only me.
This is the song
That tells my story."

Water is filling the room now. Swirling around me.
I don't stop singing:

"I am free
I am only me
This is the song
That tells my story."

And in that moment, I feel her, the other Lark. We aren't fighting anymore. We've come together. Through it all, we have come to this place, this moment.

With a whoosh, water sweeps me off my feet.

The day before: infinity point

I'm holding Reid's hand, I'm kissing Alec, I'm stealing from a store, I'm standing on top of the world, I'm with Dad in the hospital ICU, I'm feeling Alec's vicelike grip, oh, everything ...

Gasp. Splash. The shock of cold water. Heart clenching.

I am back here.

I am back here.

The lake is freezing. I suck in air.

Suzanne is screaming.

There's only one life; what should I do?

Annabelle is facedown. Alec has blood all over his face. He is sinking.

I have to do something.

I swim.

Epilogue

Epilogue

This is the story that tells my song.

Are you kidding? I'm totally not going to leave you hanging there. Although I thought about that being the end of this story for a long time, it's so hard to know where to finish, where to stop. Some of you have long ago decided that I made the whole thing up — sure, you like my music, but you're not into the whole parallel-lives stuff that I sing about. Maybe you found the fact that my mom sang about it, too, really interesting, but basically this whole story was just that to you. A story.

But it isn't a story for me. What I've told you here is everything as it happened. And whether you believe it or not, Ripley style, I bet you still have a few questions. Well, I love answering questions, and I always have time for the people who love Saturday Drowning.

Here are my answers:

1.   No, Alec is not his real name. We're not in touch, but to spare him and his issues, I thought it was better to keep his name a secret. I never, ever thought I'd be the sort of girl to end up the victim of a boyfriend. Turns out there is no such thing as the sort of girl who ends up a victim. But once I'd gotten it all back together, you can be sure I didn't date Alec.

2.   Yes, he's alive. So is Annabelle. There was time to act — I just had to move. I had to choose one. And by doing so, I had enough time. Sometimes there are happy endings. Believe me, I'm telling you how it happened. None of my friends believe me, not even Reid. But that's okay.

3.   Reid and I may or may not be dating. You know we don't answer that question in public. But let me tell you, it isn't complicated.

4.   Lucy is on the other side of the world. We stay in touch — her "nanny family" is lovely. Her ashram experience in India honestly lasted eleven days — she didn't say a word for all of them.

5.   Yes, I went to counseling. My tendency to take risks was out of control even the second time around. I had to deal with that. I don't feel any shame that I wasn't coping and that my mind couldn't handle everything life was throwing at me. I feel brave for dealing with my issues — well, dealing with them as best I can. And I know my dad, his girlfriend and my friends have got my back. And yes, I, too, cannot wait for Nifty and Cole's wedding.

6.   I still don't know if my mom experienced the things I did; if she lived a parallel life, too, like the tendency to do so is genetic or something. I suspect she didn't actually split in two the way I did, but the intensity of my dream about her gives me hope that she knew. And that she knew how much I loved her. How much I love her. All my friends think the parallel-life stuff from her is just lyrics — lyrics to one of our most popular songs, true. I know that however I live my life, whatever I do, whichever choices I make, I will always have her with me. And when I miss her most of all, I hold her guitar and play the song she gave me, the one you might have heard on the radio, the one that led you to my story.

7.   If you still have questions about me or Saturday Drowning, then I'd love to hear from you. I wrote all this down because this is the story that tells you everything you need to know about our most popular and successful song, "Parallel." Thanks for being with me as I got the words down.

8.   It hasn't been the easiest story to tell. It is the hardest story to end. But it is the story that makes me, well, me.

Lark Hardy, of Saturday Drowning

Acknowledgments

There are always so many people to thank. Firstly, Jackie Kaiser, patient, wise and thoughtful as ever. Thank you, Hadley Dyer, Jane Warren and Suzanne Sutherland, each of you for valuable and extraordinary insights. Maria Golikova and Allyson Latta (my favorite copy editor ever), thank you for spotting every tiny detail, and for making this book so much better. Thank you, Stephanie Nuñez, for your patience and amazing eye. Thank you so much, Melissa Zilberberg and Susan Busse, too! And a huge thank you to everyone at HCC for your hard work and support.

Thank you, Kate, Lisa, and the fabulous team at Kids Can Press. You have all given this book a new life, and I'm so thrilled to be working with you on this beautiful edition.

Thank you, Logan, and the others who love parkour. Thank you, Shatille.

Thank you to Brenda Baker for her words and her thoughts. Thanks to my other early readers — you know who you are.

Thank you, Reena Welder; without you I actually wouldn't be able to do any of this. Thanks also to my friends and family for being so much help and so much fun as I work.

Thank you, Alison Wood. For being there when the world turned upside-down. For rewriting the songs. For being you.

My four children are an endless distraction and delight — thanks, all of you, for keeping so cheerful when I have to work.

Above all, thank you, Yann. Always and forever, I am grateful and full of love. It is toward you that I swim.

About the Author

Alice Kuipers is an award-winning, bestselling author of four previous novels, two picture books and a chapter book series. Her work has been published in 32 countries. She lives in Saskatoon, Saskatchewan, with writer Yann Martel and their four children. Find out more about her and join her free online writing course here: alicekuipers.com

WHAT ARE YOU READING NEXT?

MORE GREAT BOOKS

KCP
Loft

kcploft.com

 @KCPLoft

NEW FROM KCP LOFT

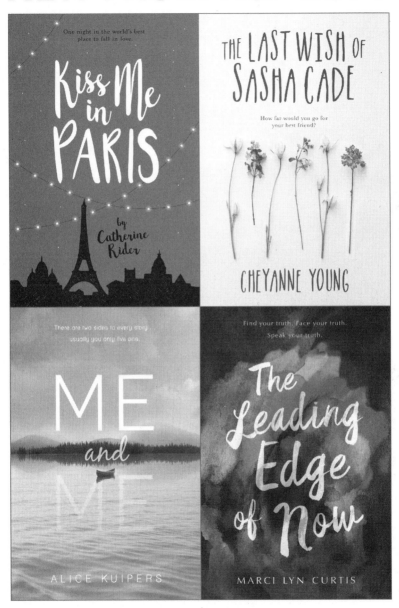

kcploft.com

@KCPLoft